PUFFIN BOOKS

GREEN SMOKE

Dragon Fairy,
Quite contrary,
How does your green smoke blow?
Through my nose
and out it goes
With smoke rings all in a row.

It was just under the cliff walk from Constantine Bay to Tre-yarnon, in a little secret cove, that Susan discovered something quite different from anything that she had ever seen before. Perhaps a 'something' is not quite the correct word, 'someone' would be more polite. His name was R. Dragon, he was 1,500 years old, and he had a great partiality for almond buns.

He was a dragon with impeccable manners, who was far too polite to eat people, and avoided meeting them because he did not like frightening them. He could also tell stories and Sue heard about the Cornish giants and fairies, and of King Arthur whom he had known very well. He taught Sue songs and took her on trips to Tintagel Castle and the Pool of Excalibur, and once to have tea with a mermaid, who told her about the country under the sea.

Altogether a charming 'someone' to discover. Further adventures with Susan and R. Dragon are told in Rosemary Manning's other Puffin Books, *Dragon in Danger*, *The Dragon's Quest* and *Dragon in the Harbour*.

Rosemary Manning was born in Dorset in 1911. After taking a Classics degree, she has had a varied career in business, teaching and lecturing.

Rosemary Manning

Green Smoke

ILLUSTRATED BY
Constance Marshall

PUFFIN BOOKS

PUFFIN BOOKS

Published by the Penguin Group
Penguin Books Ltd, 27 Wrights Lane, London W8 5TZ, England
Penguin Books USA Inc., 375 Hudson Street, New York, New York 10014, USA
Penguin Books Australia Ltd, Ringwood, Victoria, Australia
Penguin Books Canada Ltd, 10 Alcorn Avenue, Toronto, Ontario, Canada M4V 3B2
Penguin Books (NZ) Ltd, 182–190 Wairau Road, Auckland 10, New Zealand

Penguin Books Ltd, Registered Offices: Harmondsworth, Middlesex, England

First published by Constable 1957
Published in Puffin Books 1967
17 19 20 18

Printed in England by Clays Ltd, St Ives plc
Set in Monotype Garamond

for

SUSAN ELISABETH ASTLE

Contents

CHAPTER ONE

The Puff of Green Smoke

THIS is a story about a girl called Susan, or Sue for short, who went for a seaside holiday to Constantine Bay in Cornwall. Perhaps you have never been to Constantine Bay. Perhaps you have never even been to Cornwall. That won't matter at all. Just think of the rockiest rocks, the sandiest sand, the greenest sea and the bluest sky you can possibly imagine, and you will have some idea of Constantine Bay. At one end of it there is a high cliff with a lighthouse on top of it, and at the other end there is a great ridge of rocks jutting out into the sea. In between lies the yellow sand, and behind that, the sand dunes, with hummocks of tough grass, and little hot sandy paths running in and out like yellow streams. In fact, it is like all the best seaside places you have ever been to, rolled into one. Susan thought it the most beautiful and exciting place in the world. She had been there first when she was seven. Now she was eight, and she and her mother and father were just about to set off there again for their summer holidays.

This time, they travelled down to Cornwall by car very early in the morning, before it was really daylight. The birds were singing at the tops of their voices, the grass on the lawn was silvered over with dew, and the sky was pale green. A few stars were still shining overhead.

They arrived at Constantine Bay in the afternoon, in good time to rush down and look at the rocks and cliffs and make sure everything was in its right place, and of course it was, only a hundred times more glorious than Susan had remembered.

If you think it would be dull to go to the same place two years running, you will soon find out your mistake, for though rocks and cliffs may stay the same, you are always discovering new and exciting things about them. Or *in* them. For it was just under the cliff walk from Constantine Bay to Treyarnon, in a little, secret cove, that Susan discovered something quite different from anything she had ever seen before. It would be more polite to call him *Someone* rather than *Something*, and Susan met him the third day after they arrived. She was now old enough to scramble about the rocks by herself and that was how she came to find this person alone. I don't think she would ever have met him if her mother had been with her, for he did not care for people at all. He was shy and retiring in his habits. He lived in a deep black cave, under the cliff, which was not easy to get to, except at low tide. When the tide was high, the waves came right up to the entrance of the cave and made a deep booming sound, and sent clouds of spray into the air, right over the cliff top. When Susan met him, it was fairly soon after break-fast, and there were not many people about. She had climbed over the rocks, and was looking down at the black mouth of the cave, and thinking it would be fun to ask her mother to come and explore it with her, when she heard a noise very like a loud sneeze, and a little puff of green smoke came out of the cave and floated away into the air. There was a moment's silence, and then another sneeze – a very, very loud one – and another puff of smoke. Then, suddenly, a screwed-up paper bag shot out of the entrance of the cave and landed upon the sands outside.

Susan had been taught that you must not leave paper bags and orange peel and lemonade bottles about, and she was very upset at the sight of that fat, bulging paper bag, lying on the clean, untouched surface of the sand. It was not far away, and being a tidy child she decided to go and bury it out of sight, so she climbed down the rocks and walked across the sands towards it. She was just going to pick it up when there was another really colossal sneeze – KER-R-R-CHOO-OO-OO – and a thick puff of bright green smoke blew out of the cave. Susan thought to herself that it was early for people to be having picnics in caves, and sneezing, but who could it be if it wasn't picnickers? She began to dig a little hole in the sand with her fingers so that she could drop the paper bag into it. It felt as if it was full of eggshells. Susan opened the bag and peered inside. It *was* eggshells, and two or three crusts of bread, and a strong smell of pepper. Sue's nose began to tickle and she rubbed it to stop herself sneezing. Somebody had been having hard-boiled eggs for breakfast. They must have lit a fire to boil the eggs on and that was what had caused the puffs of smoke.

'People are lucky,' thought Sue, rubbing her nose hard. 'We've had dinner picnics, and tea picnics, and even, once, a supper picnic after the carnival, but we've never had a *breakfast* picnic. It would be gorgeous to eat hard-boiled eggs, cooked over a fire in a cave.'

She put the bag into the hole, covered it with sand, and was just about to go back to the rocks to ask her mother if they couldn't have a breakfast picnic the very next day, when a voice said:

'Thank you for burying my bag. You are a very tidy little girl. Quite different from most, if I may say so.'

Susan turned and looked back at the cave, but she could not see the owner of the voice.

'You shouldn't have thrown it out,' she said, sternly.

'I'm sorry,' said a humble voice. 'I didn't like to come out and bury it myself.'

'Why not?' asked Susan.

'I didn't want people to see me.'

Susan thought this was rather odd, and could only work out one reason why whoever it was couldn't come out.

'Have you been bathing and lost all your clothes?' she asked.

'No,' said the voice. 'There are other reasons.'

Susan thought for a moment.

'Shall I guess?' she said at last.

'Do,' answered the voice. 'But you'll never get the right answer. Never.'

'Are you too ugly?'

'Certainly not!' The voice sounded indignant.

'Have you – have you broken your leg and can't move?'

'All my legs are quite sound, thank you.'

'*All* your legs?' asked Susan.

'*All* my legs,' answered the voice firmly.

'It sounds as if you've got several.'

'Perhaps I have,' said the voice, and chuckled. A tiny green puff of smoke floated out on the air.

Susan was extremely interested.

'Several legs,' she murmured. 'I've only got two.'

'They must get tired on long walks, if you've only got two,' observed the voice.

'Are you a centipede?' asked Susan, suddenly remembering a creature that she knew had lots of legs.

'A centipede? Of course not,' said the voice.

'Well,' said Susan, 'my last guess is that you're so comfortable that it doesn't seem worth moving.'

'All wrong,' cried the voice triumphantly. 'All, all wrong. Ha! ha! ha! I knew you'd never guess.'

'Well, then, tell me,' said Susan, who was getting rather tired of a conversation with someone she couldn't see, who had several legs.

'If I tell you,' said the voice, and it sounded very sweet and kind, 'you won't be frightened, will you? I am so enjoying my talk with you. I haven't talked to anyone for a very, very long time.'

'I believe you're a fairy,' cried Susan, suddenly struck with this bright thought. 'A special kind of fairy with lots of legs. Perhaps a Cornish one.'

'Not a fairy,' said the voice, 'though I am Cornish. I'm a dragon.'

Susan stood quite still.

'You're not frightened, are you?' asked the voice, pleadingly. 'I have very gentle ways now.'

Susan was not quite sure that she believed that whoever it was could be a dragon. Its voice sounded so undragon-like.

'Are you really a dragon?' she asked.

'Shall I come and show you?'

'Yes,' said Susan bravely.

'Is there anyone else about? Shan't come if there is. Some people are so nasty about dragons.'

'I'm not,' said Susan. 'I'm longing to see you, and there's no one else here, so do come out.'

She had to screw up her courage to say this, because, after all, dragons can be rather alarming creatures. But Sue was stuffed full of curiosity, and she couldn't bear to go back till she had made sure whether the voice belonged to a real dragon or not. She was used to grown-ups pretending to be things that they are not.

Out of the cave came a green, scaly foot, well furnished with claws. Sue stepped back a little. It was safer to be near the rocks, she thought. Another foot appeared, and above it a large head, long like a horse's head, but bright green in colour and shining like glass. The creature had two ears and a pair of golden-yellow horns, very highly polished. His eyes were large and yellow too, like gleaming lamps. He did not look at all frightening. He seemed to have no teeth, and his wide, wide mouth was set in a charming smile.

'Shall I come out any further?' he asked.

'Well,' began Sue, and hesitated.

'I promise I won't eat you,' said the dragon. 'I never eat anyone nowadays. I've quite changed my habits.'

'Well,' said Susan again. 'I'd love to see your tail. Have you got a long one?'

The dragon turned slowly round, and Susan could see his scaly back, along the top of which were rows of yellow fins, rather like a fish's, only much bigger, and then he slowly uncoiled several yards of emerald green tail, decorated with yellow scales arranged in patterns. Laid close against his back, tidily folded, were his wings, which, like his tail, were green and scaly, and patterned with gold.

'Now are you sure I'm a dragon?' he said, and his voice sounded impatient.

'Oh, yes,' said Susan. 'I'm quite sure now. You couldn't be anything else. Why were you sneezing? Have you got a bad cold?'

'Well,' answered the dragon, 'I'll tell you. I often find bits of food left over by picnic parties, and eat them up for breakfast or supper – paste sandwiches, shrimps, apples, jam turnovers – little things like that, you know. And last night I found a bag with a hard-boiled egg in it, and a lot of eggshells. I thought I'd have it for breakfast, but when I opened the bag, I found that the horrid people had left lots of salt and pepper in it as well, and it got up my nose and made me sneeze.'

Now that the sneezes were explained, Susan quite forgot to ask about the green smoke. Suddenly she remembered her mother. She knew she ought to be getting back, but she didn't want to hurt the dragon's feelings. He seemed so eager to talk to her. So she said, as politely as she knew how:

'Would you mind very much if I went back now?'

'I should mind,' he answered at once. 'You're such a nice little girl. So different from the silly creatures that run away from me screaming.'

'Why do they scream?' asked Sue with interest, forgetting about her mother for the moment.

'They think I'm going to eat them.'

'Well, you do eat people, in stories,' said Sue.

'Oh, stories!' said the dragon scornfully. 'Stories in your human books, I suppose, written by people who never saw a dragon in their lives.'

'Have you *never* eaten people, then?' asked Susan. She was particularly interested in this question because her mother had not long ago read her a story in which a dragon nearly gobbled up an unfortunate girl who was tied to a rock.

The dragon blushed. His green cheeks turned a rosy red, so that they looked rather like half-ripe apples.

'Well,' he answered, 'I did eat some. Long ago.' He gazed far away into the distance, avoiding Susan's eyes. 'But I haven't eaten one for many centuries. I have learnt nicer habits.'

'That's a good thing,' said Susan, briskly. 'I don't want you to eat me. We couldn't go on talking if you did. Your voice would sound very funny to me if I were inside your tummy, and I don't expect you'd hear me at all.'

'We won't try,' said the dragon, hastily.

'If you *are* hungry,' said Sue, 'I've got a bun in my pocket. I was going to eat it for elevenses yesterday, but I was so excited at seeing everything again that I forgot. I'll give you half, if you like.'

'I would like it very much,' said the dragon. 'Is there any sugar on it?'

'A little,' answered Sue, dividing it in half with her sandy fingers. 'But most of it got rubbed off in my pocket.'

'Never mind,' said the dragon politely. 'Even half a bun *without* sugar on it is worth having.'

He held out his green paw for the piece of bun and took several small bites out of it.

'You've got nicer manners than me,' observed Sue, with surprise, licking her fingers which were sugary and crumby. 'Much nicer. Do tell me, dragon, did your father and mother teach you manners, or did you learn them at school? They're so polite. Like people in a book.'

'I learnt them at the court of King Arthur,' said the dragon calmly. 'That's where I learnt them. At the court of King Arthur.'

His eyes became dreamy as he repeated the words. Now Susan had been to see King Arthur's castle, which is in Cornwall at a place called Tintagel. She knew that Arthur had been a great and noble king, who lived hundreds and hundreds of years ago. Her eyes opened very wide.

'Did you know King Arthur?' she asked.

'I knew him extremely well,' answered the dragon, proudly, arching his beautiful, bright green neck.

'You are a wonderful dragon!' cried Sue, full of admiration. 'Will you tell me all about him?'

'I will if you'll come and see me again,' said the dragon. 'It would take too long now.'

'Oh, I will, I will!' cried Sue, and then suddenly remembering her mother, she added hastily: 'I really must be getting back now or Mummy will wonder what's happened to me. But of course I will come again. What shall I do? Just call out: "Dragon!" or something like that?'

'Oh, no,' said the dragon, hastily. 'That would never do. Someone might hear you. No, just come down near the cave, and if there is no one about, sing me a dragon-charming song, in a soft, careless sort of way – as if you were singing one of your nursery rhymes.'

'I don't know a dragon-charming song,' confessed Sue.

'Don't know one?' replied the dragon, with surprise. 'Well, well. How odd. You must learn one.'

'But how?' asked Sue despairingly.

'You'll find it under your pillow,' called the dragon over his shoulder, and disappeared into the cave.

Sue scrambled away quickly over the rocks, and found her mother, dozing on the beach in the sun.

'Mummy!' she cried breathlessly, 'I've found a dragon!'

'A dragon? Good!' said her mother, who was never surprised at anything.

'But he doesn't want to see you,' went on Sue. 'Only me. He doesn't like grown-up people very much.'

'Dragons never do,' said Sue's mother.

'So you won't mind if I go and see him sometimes, will you – without you, Mummy?'

'Of course not, darling,' answered her mother. So that was settled very easily.

When Susan arrived back at the cottage after they had had a picnic lunch on the beach, she rushed into her bedroom and felt under her pillow. Sure enough, there was a piece of paper – rather thick, yellow paper – and on it was written some poetry in a very odd writing, which Susan found very difficult to read. It looked like this:

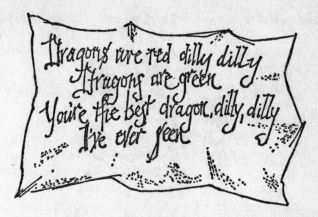

*Dragons are red dilly dilly
Dragons are green
You're the best dragon, dilly, dilly
I've ever seen*

After looking at this for some time, Susan found she could make out the words, which were these:

> *Dragons are red, dilly, dilly,*
> *Dragons are green.*
> *You're the best dragon, dilly, dilly,*
> *I've ever seen.*

When Susan had read this through slowly several times, she realized that it went to the tune of 'Lavender's blue, dilly, dilly,' so she practised singing it that night in her bath, till she had got it quite perfect, and then she planned to go straight to the cave as soon as she arrived on the beach the next day. When she came back from her bath and climbed into bed, she found that the piece of paper had gone, and though she looked everywhere she never saw it again.

CHAPTER TWO

The Story of the Flaming Dragon

NEXT morning, when her father had gone off to play golf, Susan and her mother went down to the beach.

'Would you like to rest, Mummy?' asked Sue with unusual thoughtfulness.

'I wouldn't mind,' answered her mother, rather surprised.

'You see, I want to go on a rock-climb on my own,' said Susan.

'To find the dragon?' asked her mother.

'Of course,' said Susan.

'Well, be careful,' said her mother. 'Don't let the dragon eat you, will you?'

'He never eats people nowadays,' called Susan as she ran off towards the rocks.

She was soon over the great rocky ridge which

separated her from the dragon's cave. The tide was out in
the mornings. If you have had a seaside holiday, you
probably know that the time of high tide is different
every day. Susan knew about this, and realized that the
tide would not be high till the afternoon for several days,
so that she could visit the dragon's cave safely in the
morning, when it was low. There was no one about on
the fresh clean sand of the tiny cove, so Susan ran up to
the mouth of the cave and sang, rather breathlessly:

> *'Dragons are red, dilly, dilly,*
> *Dragons are green.*
> *You're the best dragon, dilly, dilly,*
> *I've ever seen.'*

Instantly two bright lights appeared far down the cave,
like two lamps hanging from the roof. The lamps moved
towards her and she saw that they were the dragon's eyes.

'Good morning, dragon,' said Susan.

'Good morning,' answered the dragon, looking
pleased to see her. 'You remembered the dragon charm
very nicely. I thought you'd know the tune.'

'How are you this morning?' asked Susan politely.

'Very well, thank you,' answered the dragon, 'and
just the same as yesterday. Have you brought me another
bun?' and he eyed Sue's pocket rather greedily.

'Yes, I have. I thought you seemed rather hungry so
I've brought you half my elevenses bun. I ate my half
climbing over the rocks.'

It cost Susan a good deal to hand over the bag to the
dragon. It contained half a Swiss bun and Susan was particularly fond of Swiss buns.

'How delightful!' exclaimed the dragon, taking out

the half bun and looking at it all round. He nibbled elegantly at it.

'I always leave the sugar top till last,' said Susan.

'Not the way I was taught to eat a bun,' said the dragon, frowning. 'Did you tell your mother you had met me?'

'Oh, yes.'

'And I suppose she screamed and said you were never to come here again?'

'Oh, no, she didn't,' said Sue. 'She didn't do that at all. When I said I'd met a dragon, she just thought I was making up a story. I often make up stories. I don't expect grown-ups to believe them.'

'But I'm *true*,' said the dragon, rather offended.

'Oh, I know you are!' cried Sue, 'and I like you very, very much. I don't care if the grown-ups don't believe me. But I think I must ask Mummy to give me two buns for elevenses,' she added, as the dragon delicately licked the last crumbs off his claws.

'It was kind of you, really very kind and unselfish of you, to give me half your bun,' said the dragon graciously, 'and in return I will do something for you – something useful and instructive.'

'What's instructive?' asked Sue.

'Well,' said the dragon, 'I mean, I'll tell you something you ought to know – I'll *teach* you something.'

'Oh,' said Sue, rather disappointed. 'It sounds rather like arithmetic. Must it be something useful?'

'What's the use of knowing things that aren't useful?' demanded the dragon, in a surprised voice.

'Only that useful things are so dull,' answered Sue. 'Things like learning tables, and wiping one's shoes, and brushing one's teeth.'

'D'you call those *useful*?' cried the dragon. 'Oh, dear me, times have changed. Now, in my young days the things that were thought useful were things like magic, dragon-charming songs, and knowing what time the moon rises, and which berries are bad to eat, and, of course – most useful of all – stories. We were always taught stories. If you don't know lots of stories, no one will ever ask you to a party.'

'Is that what you did at your parties?' asked Sue. 'Told stories?'

'Of course,' answered the dragon. 'What do you do at yours?'

'Well, we play games, and sing, and eat buns, and jellies.'

'Oh, we did those things as well,' said the dragon. 'But the story-telling was the most important. Don't you tell stories at your parties?'

'No,' said Sue. 'I don't think we ever do.'

'And your dear father and mother,' went on the dragon. 'Don't they sit and tell each other stories in the long winter evenings?'

'I don't think so,' said Sue. 'I've never heard them.'

'Extraordinary,' said the dragon. 'I suppose none of you know any. How sad. I'd better start teaching you some good stories at once.'

'About King Arthur?' begged Susan.

'All right,' said the dragon. 'About King Arthur to start with, if you like. I'll tell you one of the early ones, since it's always best to begin at the beginning. That's the first rule of story-telling. So I'll tell you about Arthur's birth. But first, as you seem to know so little, poor child, I must explain who Merlin was. Merlin is the name of a great magician. I learnt all I know about magic from Merlin.'

'Can *you* do magic?' interrupted Susan.

'A little,' said the dragon, modestly casting down his eyes. 'But not for everyone.'

'For me?' asked Susan anxiously.

'Perhaps. We shall see. There's no need to be magical at the moment. D'you want me to go on with the story?'

'Oh, yes, please,' said Susan. 'Only you won't forget about the magic, will you? I've never known anyone who could do magic.'

'Well, if it's magic you're interested in (and very right and proper that you should be),' said the dragon, 'you should have known Merlin. He was the one for magic. Better than any of us dragons, or even fairies.'

'Couldn't we go and find him?' asked Sue.

'No, I'm afraid not,' said the dragon. 'He's gone now, with King Arthur and Sir Bedivere, and Sir Percival and all the knights of the Round Table, and all the people of those old days. He's gone to the Isle of Avalon, which is very far away.'

The dragon reached up a scaly paw and wiped his eyes. Susan didn't say anything. She could understand that it made the dragon sad to be without his old friends.

'Merlin was the most wonderful magician who ever lived,' went on the dragon, when he had recovered. 'I knew him well. His mother was a beautiful princess, but his father came from fairyland, and that was why Merlin, their child, had magic powers. When he grew up, he was able to catch and ride the wild stags. He could speak the fairy language, and the language of birds and beasts; he could tell what was going to happen in the future, and he could turn himself into anything he liked – an old man, or a pig, or a tree. The fairy people built him a splendid house in the heart of the Enchanted Forest, a house with sixty doors and seventy windows, and here he lived when he was grown up, all alone, reading his books of magic.'

'Was he a good magician?' asked Sue, 'or a bad one?'

'Oh a good one, a very good one,' answered the dragon. 'He helped the greatest king who ever lived, King Arthur. Arthur's court was in Cornwall. They liked dragons, did Merlin and Arthur. In fact,' added the dragon, proudly, 'King Arthur had a golden dragon painted on his shield.'

'A picture of you?' asked Sue, gazing open-mouthed at the dragon.

There was a long pause. The dragon was secretly longing to tell Sue that Arthur's dragon was a picture of himself, but after a struggle, he decided to tell the truth.

'No, not exactly a picture of me,' he said. 'Not a picture of one particular dragon at all. Just a dragon. Of course,' he added, 'the painter of the shield may have put one or two bits of me into it. I often fancied it had a nose rather like mine. I was about King Arthur's court a good deal. You see, dragons were mixed up in King Arthur's story. It was a dragon who gave the magic sign that Arthur was going to be born and that's the story I'm telling you. It happened this way. Are you comfortable, because it's quite long?'

'I'm quite comfortable, thank you,' said Susan. 'Please go on.'

'Well, I told you that Merlin lived in a fairy house built in the middle of a wood – the Enchanted Forest – a house with –'

'Seventy windows and sixty doors!' interrupted Sue.

'That is the one,' said the dragon. 'This was long before Arthur was born, in the days of his father, the king called Uther Pendragon. Even he had a dragon mixed up in his name, you see – Uther Pendragon. Now this King Uther loved a beautiful princess called Igraine, but he could not marry her because she was kept locked up in a strong castle. But Merlin had read in his books of magic that one day Uther would carry Igraine off from the castle and marry her, and that they would have a son and a daughter, and the magic books told him, also, that just before this happened, there would appear in the sky a splendid sign. So Merlin often looked out of his seventy windows and watched the night sky, waiting for the sign that he knew he would see in the dark, starry heavens.

'One night it was very stormy. Huge clouds spread across the moon and stars, and the wind blew them along like ships in full sail. Yet though there was a tremendous wind up in the sky, the Enchanted Forest was quite still and silent, as though it were waiting for something strange to happen. And as Merlin watched, feeling certain that this was going to be the night, he suddenly saw, far away in the north of the cloudy sky, a tiny gleam of light. It grew brighter and brighter; it turned a deep gold in colour, and then a deep red, like a glowing ruby. It became a fiery ball, and gradually it grew and grew and took on the shape of a flaming dragon, spreading right across the sky. The fiery dragon opened its long fiery jaws, and out darted two beams of light. One of them disappeared far into the west, into the shadows of the night sky, and the other came to rest on the distant eastern hills.

'Merlin then ran quickly down his long staircase, and

flew on invisible wings into the night. He knew that the dragon was hanging in the sky just above the great castle of King Uther Pendragon. He changed himself into an old man as he walked up the grassy path to the castle gates. A long, white beard fell down from his chin to his knees, his hair turned white, and his rich embroidered clothes were changed into a tattered brown tunic and a long dark-grey cloak, which reached to his ankles. In his hands, now knotted and old, he held a rough staff. Stooping, and walking slowly, Merlin went up to the castle gates and knocked loudly with his staff, three times. Above him, in the dark sky, stretched the form of the flaming dragon, and the light from it glowed on the towers and battlements of the castle. The servants, the grooms and the pages, the guards and the porters, had already seen the dragon, and were terrified. They did not at first dare to open the castle gates for fear that the creature would swoop down from the sky and enter the castle and perhaps kill them all. But Merlin knocked again even more loudly, and at last a trembling porter came to the door.

' "What do you want?" he stammered.

' "Lead me into the presence of King Uther!" cried Merlin, and his voice was so firm and commanding that the porter did not dare to disobey. He unlocked the castle gates with shaking hands and Merlin was led in through the stone passages, and across the great courtyard, into the presence of King Uther himself, who sat alone in his throne room, pale with fear, watching through the open, un-curtained windows the tremendous glare of light in the sky.

'Uther saw the old man approaching, white-haired and stooping.

' "Who are you?" he demanded, angry that his porters should have allowed a stranger into the throne room, unannounced.

' "I am Merlin," cried the old man, and as he threw back his brown cloak, his beard and white hair vanished away, leaving him the handsome, half-fairy-like man that he really was.

' "Merlin!" cried the king. "Ah, Merlin, how glad I am that you have come to me this terrible night. You alone can tell me the meaning of the sign in the sky. What is this dragon? Is some evil about to befall me and my people?"

' "No evil thing," answered Merlin. "Nothing but good, for this dragon is the sign I have long waited for. To you and the beautiful princess Igraine shall be born a son. He is the bright beam of light that springs from the jaws of the dragon and shines into the eastern sky, for your son shall be as bright and fair as the light of the morning in the east."

' "And the other ray of light?" asked the king. "The other ray?"

' "The other ray, which breaks into seven smaller rays, and shines into the west," said Merlin, "will be a daughter. She will be a princess, but more than a princess, for she will have fairy powers, and she will have seven fairy children, and they will teach the people of the west to sing the songs that only the fairies know and sing."

' "I cannot understand," said King Uther. "Am I to marry the fair Igraine, who even still is locked in her castle where I have not entered for many a long year?"

' "You shall have her for your bride," answered Merlin. "I will help you to win her and you shall marry her, in a year from this day. But in return you must make me a promise."

' "I will promise anything," said the king eagerly.

' "Then promise," said Merlin in a solemn voice, stretching out his hand, "promise that when your son is born you will hand him over to me to carry away to a place where you will never see him. He shall be brought up in the house of a noble knight who shall never know that he is a king's son."

' "I promise," said King Uther, and clasped Merlin's hand in his.

'There was a roll of thunder, and the King and Merlin stood at the open arch of the window and looked up into the sky. The great dragon closed its jaws, and the two beams of light faded away. It stretched out its golden wings and struck them three times together, and the sky was filled with thunder. Then it sped through the night in a blaze of fire.'

'Like a shooting star?' breathed Sue.

'Yes,' said the dragon, 'only a hundred times bigger and brighter. And all happened as Merlin foretold. The King married Igraine, and a boy was born, and the very day that he was born, the King handed him over to the care of Merlin, as he had promised. That baby boy was King Arthur.'

'But you didn't explain how Uther rescued her from the castle,' objected Sue. 'You said Igraine was locked up. How did she get out?'

'Oh, the usual way we did things then,' said the dragon airily. 'By magic. Merlin worked it.'

'That was a glorious story,' said Sue with a sigh of contentment. 'Now go on and tell me about Arthur.'

'Dear me,' said the dragon. 'What an appetite you've got.'

'Appetite?' said Susan. 'D'you mean I'm greedy? I did give you my bun, you know.'

'An appetite for stories, I meant,' said the dragon.

'Well, you've got an appetite for buns, I rather think,' retorted Susan, remembering what had happened to her elevenses.

'Perhaps I have,' admitted the dragon. 'But I've told you a whole story in exchange for half a bun. If you want another story it will mean another bun, and a whole one this time.'

The dragon knew perfectly well that Susan hadn't got another bun, and he sat back lazily, rather pleased with his remark.

'All right,' said Susan, huffily. 'Perhaps I ought to be getting back to mother anyway. Shall I see you tomorrow, dragon?'

'If you like,' answered the dragon sleepily, his eyes half closed.

'Shall I use the same dragon-charming song?'

'Unless you find another one under your pillow,' said the dragon. 'It depends how I feel. If I wake up (and here he gave a tremendous yawn) IF I . . . yow-ow-ow-orrrrrr-ugh! (he yawned again) wake up later on, I might send you a different one. I like variety. And that,' he added, suddenly opening one eye and fastening it upon Susan, 'that applies to buns too.'

'I don't quite understand,' said Sue. 'What's that word you said?'

'Variety?'

'Yes, that word.'

'It means, I don't like too much of the same thing, twice or three times running.'

'Oh, I see,' said Susan. 'You mean you'd like me to use a different charm sometimes.'

'Yes,' said the dragon. 'And a different bun.'

'I don't know about the bun,' answered Susan, doubtfully. 'Mummy buys them.'

'Ask your dear mother to buy you an almond bun tomorrow. I am very partial to the flavour of almonds.'

'Well, I'll see,' said Susan.

'No bun, no story,' murmured the dragon, lying back again and closing his eyes.

'I will try,' said Susan, 'but won't you ever tell me stories unless I pay for them with buns?'

There was a short pause. Then the dragon smiled and waved one paw towards Susan.

'Don't mind me,' he said. 'I'm not as greedy as I sound. I am your kind old dragon who loves you, and I *will* tell you stories, even without buns.'

'Dear dragon!' cried Susan and blew him a kiss as she ran away across the sands.

The dragon placed a loud kiss upon his own scaly paw and blew it after her. The kiss wafted across the sands, on a puff of green smoke, and rose slowly into the air over the top of the cliff, where some picnickers saw it and thought it very extraordinary.

'Green smoke!' cried one of them. 'Goodness gracious!'

'Wherever has that come from?' cried another.

Down below them, the dragon gave a throaty laugh, and popped into his cave before they could see him.

'Most odd,' the picnickers said to each other, as they

peered over the edge of the cliff, waving their sandwiches in their hands.

'There's a little girl!' cried one, pointing at Susan, who was scrambling over the rocks below them.

Susan looked up at their red, worried faces.

'It was only a dragon's kiss!' she called out, laughing at them, for she knew that they would never believe her. And of course they didn't. They went back to their jam tarts and lemonade and cherry cake, and puzzled over that green smoke for the rest of the day. One of them even wrote to the newspapers about it.

That evening when Susan looked under her pillow, there was another yellowish piece of paper and on it was written:

> 'Dragon-fairy,
> Quite contrary,
>   How does your green smoke blow?
> Through my nose
> And out it goes
>   With smoke rings all in a row.'

'How funny!' thought Susan. 'He calls himself a fairy. But I suppose he has to do that to make it rhyme with contrary. That's an easy one, anyway. I can sing it to the tune of "Mary, Mary, quite contrary." '

And she practised it in her bath several times over. When she came back to her room, the piece of paper had gone. She looked under the bed, and in the waste-paper basket, but she never found it.

CHAPTER THREE

How Saint Petroc Tamed the Dragon

As it happened, Sue couldn't go and see the dragon next day, as her mother and father wanted to take a picnic lunch out in the car. They all went over to Bedruthan Steps, and spent the day there, and explored new rocks and caves and cliffs, and Susan enjoyed herself so much that she hardly had time to think about the dragon at all after the first ten minutes of wishing he was there too.

But the following day, she hurried down to the beach and sang her new dragon-charming song:

> *'Dragon-fairy,*
> *Quite contrary,*
> *How does your green smoke blow?*
> *Through my nose*
> *And out it goes*
> *With smoke rings all in a row.'*

There was a slight scuffling in the cave and then silence. 'Dragon!' called Sue. There was no reply. She went nearer the cave and sang the rhyme again, a little louder.

At last the dragon's voice said, rather crossly: 'Why didn't you come yesterday?'

'I'm sorry,' said Susan. 'I wanted to come, but Mummy and Daddy took me out for the day.'

'Oh,' said the dragon, coldly.

'Please don't be cross, dear dragon,' pleaded Sue. 'Do come out and be nice.'

'I don't need to come out,' said the dragon. 'I can be nice in my cave.'

'I want to see you.'

'Oh, well.' The dragon put his head out. He was looking rather pale green and had black rings under his eyes. His ears hung limply and his yellow horns had no shine.

'Oh, dear dragon!' cried Sue. 'You don't really look a bit well. Are you feeling bad? Is there a dragon doctor we could send for?'

Her anxious interest immediately made the dragon feel much better. He brightened a little, and came further out of his cave towards Sue. He even gave a very small smile.

'The truth is,' he said, 'I had rather a horrid day yesterday. Some nasty trippers came and poked about in my cave, and then I lost the little parcel of food I'd saved for my lunch, and *then* you didn't come, so I never got my bun, and *then* I caught my tail in between two rocks and pinched it, and *then* ...'

He began to sound quite tearful.

'Oh, *poor* dragon!' said Sue, soothingly.

'You know how it is,' went on the creature, looking at her with a woebegone expression. 'Some days everything seems to go wrong.'

'People call it getting out of bed on the wrong side,' said Susan. 'I do it sometimes.'

'I suppose I could call it getting off a rock on the wrong side,' said the dragon, and began to laugh. Susan laughed too.

'I feel better now,' said the dragon. 'Tell me where you went yesterday.'

So Susan told him all about the picnic and the long steps down the cliff to the bay at Bedruthan, and how exciting and steep they were.

'Now you tell me things you've done,' said Sue. 'You must have done lots of things more exciting than climbing down Bedruthan Steps. Did you enjoy doing things like that when you were young – when you were a kind of dragon cub?'

'When I was young,' said the dragon, 'before King Arthur's time, that was, I was very, very wicked.'

'Oh, dragon!' cried Sue, reproachfully. 'Were you really? What – you ate people and things like that?'

'Ate them right up, bones and all,' said the dragon, sorrowfully. 'And their cattle and sheep as well.'

'How horrid of you! I'm glad I didn't know you then.'

'So am I. You wouldn't have liked me at all.'

'When did you stop being wicked?' asked Susan.

'Well, there lived at that time a good, holy man – a Saint, they called him, which I think means someone who is extra kind and noble. There were lots of them about in Cornwall in those days. Perhaps people were better than they are now. There was a Saint Enodoc and Saint Agnes, and Saint Samson, and I don't know how many more. This one's name was Saint Petroc. Everyone in Cornwall knows him. There are churches called Saint Petroc's Church, after him, and I'm always pleased when I see one, because it reminds me of him and how he stopped me being a wicked dragon.'

'Well, do tell me what happened,' said Sue impatiently. 'How did he stop you being wicked?'

'I was living in a marsh at the time,' said the dragon, in a gloomy voice, 'living in a dark, damp, smelly marsh and just being wicked. Everybody hated me, and at last the poor people living round about sent a message to Saint Petroc begging him to come and get rid of me. I think they hoped that he would strike me dead, or turn me to stone, or something. He arrived one afternoon, with two of his friends, Samson and Wethnoc, both very good men, and I thought to myself in my wicked way (laughing heartily): "Here's three more of these foolish human beings come to try and kill me. If I roar loud enough, they'll scream and run away, and maybe I can catch the slowest of them and eat him." So I let out a terrible roar and belched smoke and flames at them. I must say that Samson and Wethnoc seemed rather frightened. They shook and trembled. But they stood their ground. They didn't run away. Instead, they knelt down and prayed. "Ho! Ho!" thought I. "You just go on kneeling there and I'll soon gobble you up, when I've finished with this Saint Petroc." And I let out another roar specially for him. But then I saw a strange thing. Saint Petroc came towards me, smiling so sweetly, and holding out his hand. There was a lump of sugar in it. He called out: "Come along, then! Good dragon! Good boy! Come to master!"

'And suddenly I thought how lonely I was living in

that horrible marsh and being wicked, and hated by everybody, and how pleasant it would be to have people calling me "Good Dragon", and holding out their hands with lumps of sugar, so I got up and walked towards Saint Petroc, without breathing another flame. Saint Petroc was wearing a long, thick gown, with a girdle, and while I was chewing up the sugar lump, he took off the girdle and tied it round my neck and I walked behind the three of them down the road, as meek and mild as a sheep.

'As we approached the town, we saw a huge procession of people coming out of it, and when the first few of them reached us, they stopped, and told Saint Petroc that the king's son had died and that they were coming out to bury him. There were three hundred soldiers marching in file, and then a great ox-cart, on which was laid the dead body of the king's young son, and that was being pulled by forty of the townspeople. Now when I saw all those human beings weeping and wailing, I remembered how often I had frightened them, and eaten up their friends and relations, and I felt sorry for my wicked ways, so I wept too. I thought how stupid I had been to frighten these good people, when what I really wanted was to be liked by them, so I decided that I would do something to please them. I sat back on my haunches and blew a beautiful smoke ring, and then, closing my jaws slightly, I blew another, smaller ring, right through the first.'

'Oh, do do it now!' cried Susan.

'Not in the middle of the story,' said the dragon, severely. 'I might do it at the end.

'Now, wouldn't you have thought that they'd have liked those smoke rings? Not a bit of it. They were terrified. They thought I was just about to rush upon them and gobble them up. They flung down their swords and spears and uttered loud shrieks, and the whole funeral procession ran back towards the town, and we were left alone on the highway with the body of the young prince. Saint Petroc handed the end of the girdle which was my leash to his friend Samson. "Hold Brother Dragon for a moment," he said, and then he went over to the ox-cart and laid his hands upon the shoulders of the young dead prince, and marvellous to tell, the young man sat up, alive and well again. At that, the townspeople, who had been watching from a distance, came running along the road again, and crowded round Saint Petroc, and some of them even patted me timidly, when they saw how gently I sat there at the end of Petroc's girdle. I smiled at them, and waved my tail slowly from side to side, to make them think I was a kind of over-sized dog.

'"Now, dragon, you are to go and live down upon the seashore, in a cave for your home, and never again are you to trouble good people, and they will never trouble you, but you will all live peaceably together and be much happier," said Saint Petroc kindly, and he untied my girdle.

'So I promised him that I would never again be wicked, and I walked away towards the seashore, and many of the people waved their pocket-handkerchiefs at me, and I waved my tail back at them. Since then I've always lived in caves by the seashore. Saint Petroc was quite right to send me to live there. It's the best place in the world to live.'

'Oh, you are lucky,' sighed Sue. 'I wish I could live by the sea always and always.'

'You'd better be wicked and eat people,' suggested the dragon, 'and perhaps Saint Petroc will come and catch you.'

'Did you ever see Saint Petroc again?' asked Sue.

'Once,' answered the dragon. 'I was rootling for some juicy shoots at the bottom of a tree, when a splinter of wood broke off and went into my eye.'

'Poor dragon!' cried Sue. 'Did it hurt terribly?'

'It was horribly painful,' said the dragon. 'I didn't know what to do. Then I remembered Saint Petroc, and I thought: "I'm sure he could cure me." He only lived about twenty miles away, so I found my way as best as I could across country to the place where he lived, and I roared with pain, and great tears rolled out of my eyes. But Saint Petroc was away, and no one could help me. True, one of the monks bathed my wounded eye, and they let me lie on the steps of their church and fed me with bread and milk, but no one knew what to do to cure my poor eye, which was now quite blind. On the third day, I heard a step which I recognized, and the next moment, there was Saint Petroc beside me.

' "Why, Brother Dragon!" he cried, and stroked my head. "What's happened to you?"

'He examined my eye carefully, and thought for a moment. Then he turned to the monk who had been bathing it, and said:

' "This poor beast is half blinded. Take a jug of the spring water and mix it with some of the dust from the floor of our church, and pour this over the dragon's eye."

'Then he patted my head again and went his way. He was a very busy man. And the monk did as Saint Petroc had told him, and as soon as he poured the water over my head and into my bad eye, the splinter of wood dropped out, and I could see as well as before. So I rubbed the monk up and down with my head, just to show I was grateful, and, waving my tail joyfully, I walked the twenty miles back to my seashore again.'

'Is that the end?' asked Sue.

'The end of *that* story,' said the dragon, 'and a very important story too.'

'Now will you blow me two smoke rings? I've never seen you blow out smoke – at least, yes, I have. When you were sneezing, the first time I met you.'

'And then I blew you a kiss,' the dragon reminded her.

'Oh, yes, of course! And those people on the cliff saw it and wondered whatever it was. They did look so funny peering over. Do please blow me some rings.'

'All right,' said the dragon obligingly.

He puffed out his cheeks and pursed his lips into a huge O. Out popped a perfect ring. Then he pursed his lips up a little, blew out another smaller ring, and it sailed out into the air right through the first one.

'Oh, lovely!' cried Susan. 'How clever you are! I must ask Daddy if he can do it when he's smoking.'

'He won't be able to,' said the dragon at once. 'It takes hundreds of years' practice to do it. Now I want to go to sleep, and it's time you were going back to your dear mother.'

'I expect it is,' said Susan. 'Will you just blow me two more rings?'

'Just another couple,' said the dragon.

This time, he blew them so quickly that the second ring shot through the first like an arrow, and coiled itself round the neck of a large gull, which looked very surprised, uttered a shriek of dismay, and flew away, with the green smoke ring curled round its neck like a muffler.

'There,' said the dragon, proudly. 'It's a long time since I did that.'

'Thank you,' said Susan. 'It was wonderful. And you're a very clever dragon. The cleverest in the world. What charm shall I use tomorrow when I come?'

'Just use whichever you like. Good–bye. I'm sleepy.'

'Oh!' cried Susan, turning back. 'I quite forgot the bun.'

'Goodness!' said the dragon. 'So did I. Have you got one for me?'

'Here you are,' said Susan. 'It's an almond one.'

The dragon was very pleased.

'I'll save it, and have it for my dinner,' he said, and waved good-bye as he disappeared into his cave.

CHAPTER FOUR

I'm for Tintagel Castle!

'I WOULD love to see lots of places,' said Sue, the next day, when she had sung her new dragon-charming song and the dragon had come bounding out of his cave, looking extremely bouncing and energetic.

'What places?' he said, scratching the back of his ear with his green claw.

'Well, there's Iceland and India, and Honolulu, and Salisbury Cathedral.'

'Well, you probably will,' said the dragon. 'People seem to travel about a lot nowadays.'

'I can never see them all,' said Sue. 'It would take too long.'

'It's a pity you're not a fairy,' observed the dragon. 'Then you would only have to say: "I'm for Honolulu!" (wherever that may be) and you'd be there, and when you wanted to come home, you'd only have to say: "I'm for Constantine Bay!" and there you'd be, tucked up in bed and nobody a penny the wiser. It might work if you could even *meet* some fairies, but that's not so likely these days. They keep themselves well hidden. I knew of a boy once, a farmer's boy he was. He lived over at Portallow, and one fine day he was sent out by his mother to do some shopping in the neighbouring village. On the way home, it grew dark, and suddenly he saw in the field over the hedge a number of tiny lights flickering to and fro. He peered over the gate, and there to his astonishment were the piskies, playing games in the shelter of a big rock. Suddenly he heard their fairy voices call out: "I'm for Portallow Green!" I don't know why, but he thought he'd say the same, so he shouted it out so that all the owls could hear him: "I'm for Portallow Green!" And there he was on the green of his own village, surrounded by a host of laughing piskies. He heard them lift up their voices and cry out: "I'm for Seaton Beach!" and quick as lightning, he shouted out, too: "I'm for Seaton Beach!" and there he was, among the piskies again, on the sands at Seaton, dancing about in the moonlight, and the piskies chasing him round the rocks and having a high old time.

'Suddenly they stopped playing, and this time they called out: "I'm for the King of France's cellar!"

'"I'm for the King of France's cellar!" shouted the farmer's boy, hardly knowing whether he was on his head or his heels. In the shake of a duck's tail, there they all were in the dark cellars of the King of France himself, surrounded by great barrels of wine, and casks of cider. The piskies unlocked a fine old chest of carved wood, and drew out gold and silver cups, and they opened the barrels and casks and filled all the cups. Then they sat drinking and telling stories till the farmer's boy's head was going round and round and his eyes were popping out. At last they all got up, yawning, and cried, sleepily: "I'm for Portallow Green!" The farmer's boy looked mazily round him, and picked up a fine silver goblet. "I'm not going without this!" said he. Then he stuffed it into his pocket, and cried: "I'm for Portallow Green!" and there he was, back in his own home and not yet time to go to bed.

'"You've been quick," said his mother.

'"Quick?" repeated the boy. "Quick, mother? Why, I've been half over the world since I last saw you. I've been to Seaton Beach and I've been to the King of France's cellar, with the piskies."

'"Stuff and nonsense!" said his mother. "Eat up your porridge and get yourself to bed."

'"If you don't believe me, mother," said the boy, "take a look at this." And with that, he pulled the goblet out of his pocket. There were blazing jewels round the rim, and on the base of it was cut the crest of the King of France. The silver cup is kept in the family to this day, I believe. I saw it myself a few hundred years ago.'

'That's a lovely story,' said Sue. 'I wish things like that happened nowadays.'

'I thought you had your wonderful aeroplanes, and your wonderful telephones, and your wonderful wire-lesses,' said the dragon, rather disagreeably. 'These bits of newspapers I pick up – oh, I taught myself to read ages ago, to give myself something to do – these bits of newspapers that I find wrapped round the sandwiches and the shrimps, are always bragging about the wonderful things you human beings can do. What do you want with magic?'

'I think I'd rather have the magic and the fairies,' said Susan, humbly.

'A pity more people don't agree with you. You can have your aeroplanes as far as I'm concerned. Nothing but noise. That's one of the blessings of magic. Always so *quiet*. There goes an aeroplane now,' he added angrily, as one zoomed across the sky. 'I shall have to make some seaweed ear plugs if they get much noisier.'

'I suppose *we* couldn't go somewhere by magic, like the boy in the Portallow Green story?' asked Susan.

'I don't know,' said the dragon slowly and thoughtfully. 'It's a long time since I did any magic of that kind.'

'Couldn't we find some fairies to do it?'

'I doubt it,' said the dragon. 'They've mostly gone to live over in Ireland and the faraway Scottish islands. Not so many trippers there, poking and prying. If you did happen to meet one here in Cornwall, it would be very shy. I don't think it would do any magic for you. You'd have trouble enough to get it even to talk to you.'

'*You* do the magic,' said Sue. 'I'm sure you can.'

'I suppose I could try,' said the dragon. 'Where do you particularly want to go?'

'To Tintagel!' shrieked Sue in excitement. 'To Tintagel! To Arthur's castle!'

'All right,' said the dragon, 'we can but try. Don't be disappointed, though, if it doesn't work. Get on my back and hold on tight. Are you ready?'

'Yes,' answered Susan, climbing between two of the dragon's fins, and holding on as tight as she could to his scaly back. His skin was hard and shiny, like the leather seat of a car.

'Dig your feet in,' ordered the dragon. 'You won't hurt me. Go on.'

So Susan dug her feet into the dragon's sides.

'NOW!' cried the dragon. 'I'm for Tintagel Castle!'

'I'm for Tintagel Castle!' shouted Sue, breathlessly.

There was a moment's pause.

'Won't it work?' asked Susan, anxiously.

'Wait a moment,' answered the dragon. 'I think it's going to. Just let's say it again. I'M FOR TINTAGEL CASTLE!' he bellowed, and blew a great gust of green smoke from his nostrils.

'I'm for Tintagel Castle!' shrieked Sue at the top of her voice.

An old gentleman walking along the top of the cliff above heard the noise, looked over, and to his astonishment saw what he thought was a green aeroplane rise very quickly from the beach and sail away into the sky. He stood looking after it with his mouth open, and nearly fell over the cliff because he wasn't looking where he was going.

Meanwhile, Susan and the dragon were sailing smoothly through the air, over the coast of Cornwall. They passed right over the Trevose Lighthouse, which Susan could just see from the beach, and then over the great river mouth of Padstowe, across which there is a ferry boat which carries people from side to side about every twenty minutes.

'There's the ferry!' cried Susan. 'I've been backwards and forwards on that ferry lots of times. It's lovely.'

'Not so lovely as sailing through the air,' said the dragon.

'Oh, no, of course not,' said Susan. 'All the same,

ferry boats *are* lovely,' she added, not willing to let the dragon think that he was the only wonderful thing in the world.

'There's Port Isaac,' said the dragon, pointing with his claw to a small village below them, which was built right up the side of a steep cliff.

'The houses look like birds perching on the ledges,' said Susan as they swooped low over the town.

The dragon blew several smoke rings, which trailed behind them. They could see people at Port Isaac pointing excitedly at them.

'They think I'm an aeroplane. Ha! Ha!' laughed the dragon, and blew another ring. 'They've never seen an aeroplane blowing smoke rings before. I expect they'll write to their newspapers about it. People always write to newspapers about things. I can't think why. They'd

do far better to use them up in stories. Think what a good story this would make to tell over the fire on a winter's evening. Once upon a time there was an aeroplane which could blow green smoke rings ... Ah, there's Tintagel!'

'It looks quite small from here,' said Susan. 'Like a toy castle. Look, there are lots of people.'

'Yes, I see them,' said the dragon, gloomily. 'I suppose you want to go right down, though what the people will say when they see me, I can't imagine.'

'I'll tell them how nice you are,' said Susan.

'That won't make any difference,' said the dragon. 'They'll either think I'm funny and want to put me in a circus, or else they will think I'm dangerous, and put me in a zoo. Neither prospect is at all pleasing to me. People are so stupid about dragons.'

'Well, don't let's go down there, then,' said Susan. 'It's lovely up here, and after all, we've a better view of the castle than they've got down there, haven't we?'

'Sensible child,' said the dragon, instantly becoming more cheerful.

'You're sure you won't get tired, flying about up here?'

'I'll hover,' said the dragon. 'Like a hawk.'

He stretched his large wings out to their fullest extent, and beat them up and down gently. Susan found that they were staying still over the same spot. It was a delicious sensation, hovering in mid-air, and looking down over the broken towers and turrets of Tintagel. The castle stood high up on a cliff which jutted out into the sea. The water swirled round the foot of the cliff, underneath the castle, like dark blue silk.

'Tell me more about King Arthur,' begged Susan.

'Well, he lived there, in that great castle. Not that very castle that you see, but one rather like it, hundreds and hundreds of years ago. A castle with grey stone walls, thick and strong, and mighty towers from which the watchmen could see for miles over land and sea, and spy out the enemy coming.'

'Did Arthur always live here?' asked Sue.

'Not all the time,' answered the dragon. 'He moved about, fighting his enemies and seeking adventure, and he held his court in many places besides Tintagel – at Camelot, for instance, and at Caerleon, in Wales.'

'Have you ever been to Wales?' asked Sue.

'Once. I swam there across the Bristol Channel.'

'What did you do in Wales?'

'I learnt Welsh,' said the dragon unexpectedly. 'Dyma amswer braf yr ym yn cael!' (If you say it like this it will sound right; dimma amser brav er im in kyle.)

'Oh, what does that mean?' cried Sue, enchanted with the strange sound of the language, and, of course it sounded even stranger up there in the sky, with seagulls wheeling round them, and the sea heaving so far beneath them, and the people moving about among the ruins of the castle like a host of ants.

'It means: what a lovely time we're having.'

'Oh, we are,' sighed Sue. 'So lovely I can hardly believe I'm really here. Tell me some more about Arthur.'

The dragon moved his wings, and they flew a little way inland, and looked at the castle from a different position. They could now see the long path that led up the hill to it. It was black with people, crawling along it like an army on the march.

'King Arthur,' went on the dragon, 'had many knights in his service. They sat in the castle around a huge table. They sat in deep wooden chairs, and on the back of each chair was the name of the knight, in letters of gold. Sir Bedivere was there, and Sir Lancelot, and Sir Gawain, Sir Percival and Sir Gareth, and many more, and there were tales told of all of them – so many that I couldn't tell them all to you in a year. They were called the Knights of the Round Table.'

'Couldn't you tell just *one* story, about just *one* knight?'

'Perhaps I could,' said the dragon, 'but not today. To tell the truth, my wings are getting tired. I think we ought to be flying home.'

'And what about Mummy?' cried Sue, suddenly remembering that her mother had no idea where she was. 'Won't she be getting worried?'

'No,' answered the dragon. 'Because when you get back, she won't know you've been away more than a few minutes, just over the rocks and back. That's one thing about magic: it all happens in a flash, so that ordinary people don't know you've not been there.'

'Like the boy who went to Seaton Beach and the King of France's cellar?' asked Sue.

'Like that,' answered the dragon, and started to beat his great wings like a bird.

'Good-bye!' cried Sue. 'Good-bye, Tintagel! I shall see you again.'

But as the grey towers slowly faded into the green of the cliffs, and cliffs and sea melted into a blue haze behind them, she thought: I shall see Tintagel again when I come with Mummy and Daddy, but it won't, it *can't*, ever look the same, seeing it from the ground. It will never look so huge and so old and so magic as it did when I saw it from above, in the air, on the back of a dragon. And she stroked the dragon's ears fondly.

'Don't! You're tickling me!' he said and wriggled. 'I might drop you, and that would be a misfortune, would it not?'

Susan agreed that it would, and kept very still.

Soon they passed over the Padstowe river mouth again and the ferry was halfway across the harbour, much as it had been when they had first seen it. The people in it looked up and Susan could see them pointing and waving their hats and getting very excited. The ferry boat rocked to and fro and one of the people fell into the water and had to be fished out by the ferryman, with the aid of a boathook.

'Ha! ha!' laughed the dragon, heartlessly. 'Ho! Ho!'

'Oh, poor thing!' cried Susan, whose heart was softer.

'He fell right in. Still, he's all right. They've rescued him. He's back in the ferry boat.'

'That'll give him something to talk about,' said the dragon. 'It ought to last him the rest of his life, that story. In fact, he ought to be very grateful to us. He'll be asked to every party in the neighbourhood for years to come, to tell his story of how he fell out of the Padstowe ferry boat because he saw a green dragon sailing across the sky with a little girl on his back. That story's worth its weight in gold.'

Trevose lighthouse came into sight below them, and then the yellow sands of Constantine Bay, and there they were in a few minutes, landing outside the cave. Susan thanked the dragon and kissed his scaly cheek.

'You are a wonderful dragon,' she murmured.

'I *am* rather proud of myself,' he answered. 'It's several years since I did that piece of magic, and never in my life have I done it with a little girl on my back.'

'Was I dreadfully heavy?'

'You seemed to get heavier as time went on. I expect I'll have a stiff back tomorrow.'

'Oh, dear,' said Susan, feeling rather guilty, and wishing she were lighter.

'Never mind,' the creature went on, 'it was worth it. I enjoyed seeing Tintagel again. I lived near there for many years. It brings back old memories. Happy memories.'

'Well, I shall always remember Tintagel as the most wonderful place I've ever seen,' said Sue. 'But most of all, I'll remember that I saw it from the back of a dragon and the most gorgeous dragon that ever was.'

The dragon looked very pleased at this speech.

'Good-bye!' called Susan. 'I must be getting back to mother now.'

'We've never had our bun this morning,' said the dragon, suddenly.

Sue hesitated for a moment, and then walked back to the cave.

'You can have all of it, dragon,' she said, extracting it from her pocket.

'I thought your mother gave you two buns,' said the dragon, hopefully.

'She forgot today,' said Sue. 'But do have all of it. Really. You ought to, after flying all that way.'

'Well, I must admit I'm hungry,' said the dragon. 'But I don't like to eat all your bun.'

'I expect Mummy will have some biscuits with her,' said Sue.

'In that case, I will,' said the dragon, and ate the bun, rather faster than he usually did, and with less elegance.

Sue saw it disappearing and felt very hungry herself.

She said good-bye to the dragon again, and hurried back over the rocks to her mother.

'Have you any biscuits, Mummy?' she demanded, flinging herself down on the hot sand, like a dog.

'Biscuits?' repeated her mother. 'What's happened to your bun?'

'I gave it to the dragon.'

'That dragon!' said her mother, severely. 'Now you want biscuits for the dragon, I suppose?'

'No, they're for me. We were both rather hungry. You see, we've been to Tintagel.'

'Oh,' said her mother. 'Daddy and I were thinking

of taking you there for a picnic one day. Will you mind going again?'

'Oh, no,' answered Sue. 'I'd like to see it from the ground again, like we did last year. The dragon and I only saw it from the air. We didn't come down and land.'

'Oh, I see,' said Sue's mother. 'In that case, you'd better have another biscuit. I'm sure flying to Tintagel and back has made you hungry, hasn't it?'

Which shows what an understanding mother she was.

CHAPTER FIVE

The Story of King Arthur's Sword

NEXT day, Susan was filled with delicious hopes that the dragon would take her to some other exciting place.

'I think it would be nice to take a picnic, then we shouldn't have to hurry back because the dragon was getting hungry,' thought Sue to herself, as she was getting up.

'Mummy, d'you think the dragon and I could have a picnic?' she asked after breakfast.

'Well,' answered her mother. 'It's not a good idea to eat too much in the middle of the morning. What exactly did you want for your picnic?'

'Oh, orangeade for one thing. Buns, biscuits and perhaps bananas.'

'Well, look, darling,' said her mother. 'Suppose I put you one bun, one chocolate biscuit and one banana and one bottle of orangeade into the little basket – would that do?'

'What about the dragon?' demanded Sue, who knew the dragon's appetite.

'I think he'd like it best if you shared with him.'

'Couldn't he have just one chocolate biscuit to himself?' begged Sue.

'All right, darling,' said her mother, and she put one almond cake in a bag, two chocolate biscuits into another, and packed them, with a banana and a small orangeade bottle, into Sue's shopping basket. Then she and Sue went off to the beach together. Sue's mother settled herself against a rock and took out her knitting.

'You won't be too long, will you?' she said.

'I'll be back in – two shakes of a duck's tail!' cried Sue, gaily, remembering what the dragon had said about magic time being quite different from that kept by ordinary people.

'Have a nice picnic!' called out her mother as Sue scrambled away over the rocks towards the dragon's cave.

'I'll give your love to the dragon!' shrieked Susan and disappeared.

She climbed the far rocks and went over to the cave. She put down the basket and sang the old dragon-charming song:

> *'Dragons are red, dilly, dilly,*
> *Dragons are green.'*

The dragon came slowly and stiffly out of the cave, yawning and rubbing his eyes.

'Overslept today,' he said, rather crossly. 'So stiff and worn out after all my hard work yesterday.'

'O dragon!' began Sue.

'What do you mean – O dragon?' he said, rather nastily, glaring at Sue with a red and suspicious eye.

'Well, it was just a way of saying "Hullo". I thought "Hullo" mightn't be polite enough for a dragon, so I said "O dragon!" like they do in books.'

'I'm not in a book.'

'Oh, dear!' said Susan, with a sigh. 'Have I offended you? You do get cross quickly, dear dragon.'

Perhaps it was the 'dear dragon' that did it, but from that moment, the dragon looked better-tempered.

'Do I?' he said, beginning to smile. 'Then I will get uncross quickly, too.' He made his toothless smile even wider, so that it stretched almost into his ears on either side.

'Is that better?' he asked.

'Much better,' said Susan, relieved.

'I am always interested in your human antics,' went on the dragon. 'This addressing me as "O dragon", for instance. Does the O stand for a name? Oliver, or Osbert, or Oswald, or ... or Oleander?'

'No, no, no!' cried Susan, getting impatient. 'It's just a way of saying "Hullo", or "Good morning".'

'I see,' said the dragon, thoughtfully. 'Well, I should say "Good morning" next time. My name, if it interests you at all, begins with an R. You may therefore say: "Good morning, R. Dragon."'

'Good morning, R. Dragon,' said Sue. 'What does R. stand for?'

'That's my secret,' answered the dragon, closing his eyes tightly. 'Dragons and fairies have to keep their names secret. If we didn't, people would have all sorts of powers over us.'

'Like in Rumpelstiltskin?' suggested Sue, who remembered that the point of that story was the finding out of Rumpelstiltskin's name.

'Rumpelstiltskin?' repeated the dragon, opening his eyes again. 'Who's he? I don't know him. He can't be English.'

'He's out of a book called *Grimm's Fairy Tales*,' said Sue, 'and the story's about a girl who said she could spin flax into gold, and the king put her into his attic, and told her to spin, and of course she couldn't make a single gold thread.'

'Of course not,' said the dragon. 'I'm not surprised – foolish girl. Wool's wool and gold's gold – unless you happen to know any magic. She sounds a very stupid young woman. I hope *you* don't have any such foolish thoughts.'

'Of course I don't,' said Sue. 'Shall I go on with the story?'

'Yes,' answered the dragon. 'I shall be interested to hear what happened to this addle-pated creature.'

'A little man came and turned the wool into gold for her,' Susan continued. 'The king was so pleased that he married her. And then, you see, she promised to give up her baby to the little man, unless she could find out his name. She'd had to promise that before he would spin the wool into gold for her. Well, she thought and she thought and she thought, and she couldn't guess it, and her servants went out north and south and east and west, and *they* couldn't find it out either, till, at last, one of them heard someone singing as he danced round a fire, and d'you know what he was singing, dragon?'

'*Here we go round the Mulberry bush*' suggested the dragon.

'No!'

> *'Sally go round the sun*
> *Sally go round the moon,*
> *Sally go round the plum-tree*
> *On a Saturday afternoon?'*

'No! Oh, no!' cried Sue. 'The voice was singing:

> *"Today I'll brew and tomorrow I'll bake,*
> *And then the queen's child I will take,*
> *For little deems my royal dame*
> *That RUMPELSTILTSKIN is my name!"*

'So the servant ran home and told the girl, and when the little man came to claim the baby, she teased him, saying: "Is your name John? Is it Pugface? Is it Buttercup?" and all the silliest things she could think of, and when he was just getting angry, and reaching out his hairy little hands for the baby, she screamed out: "It's Rumpelstiltskin!" and that was the end of the little man. Now, what shall we do?' ended Susan, hopefully.

'I'll tell *you* a story,' said the dragon, sitting up.

'Oh,' said Sue, slightly disappointed. 'You wouldn't like to go somewhere exciting?'

'Not particularly,' answered the dragon, yawning. 'I've been to so many places. Now I just like staying still. You go to places if you want to,' he added rather nastily. 'Run along! All this everlasting rushing about,' he added crossly, under his breath.

'I don't want to go without you,' answered Sue, tearfully. 'And I brought a special picnic for us both.'

The dragon looked better pleased. He liked to be the centre of attraction.

'Well, then,' he said. 'You may stay with me here because I really am too tired to do any magic today, but perhaps I might feel more like it tomorrow, and you could always bring another picnic, couldn't you? Stay with me, and you may sit on my seaweed rug, and I will tell you a story, a really exciting one. Then we shall both be pleased. And we will eat the picnic afterwards.'

Susan thought privately that it was the dragon who was really getting most pleasure out of this arrangement, but she swallowed her disappointment about the magic, and, remembering that the dragon did, after all, tell very good stories, she said: 'That'll be lovely.'

The dragon looked very pleased with himself.

'Is it about Arthur?' asked Sue.

'As a matter of fact it is. It's about his wonderful sword, which was called Excalibur.'

'Why did his sword have a name?' asked Susan.

'Why not?' retorted the dragon. 'You have a name, haven't you? I don't have to address you as "Child".'

'No, but a sword is – well, it's just a thing. Mother doesn't call her kettle by a name, or her frying-pan, either.'

'Very foolish of her,' said the dragon reprovingly. 'I can't think how she gets them to cook anything for her. Remember that when you grow up. Things like to have names. It puts them in a good humour. Now, Arthur's sword was called Excalibur.'

'Please say it again,' interrupted Sue.

'Excalibur,' said the dragon, rather impatiently.

'It's a terribly difficult name to remember,' said Sue, with a heavy sigh. 'So long, and sort of awkward.'

'I don't think I shall tell you the story at all,' said the dragon, sitting back and shutting his long green jaws very tightly.

'Oh, *please*,' cried Susan. 'Please, please, please!'

'You keep interrupting,' complained the dragon. 'If I tell you stories, you must let me tell them in my own way. You mustn't stop me in the middle. I haven't any chapters. When I start a tale, it has to go on to the very end of it.'

He waved the tip of his tail slowly up and down.

'I like that sort best,' said Susan.

'Then we'll begin again,' said the dragon, and the tip of his tail became still.

'This is the story of King Arthur's sword, Excalibur. When Arthur was a young king, he loved to fight, and would always answer the challenge of any strange knight. One day, he found that a stranger had set up his tent by a fountain in Arthur's own royal forest, and this knight, whose name was Pellinore, refused to let anyone pass his tent without a fight. So Arthur rode up to him, and when the knight challenged him to combat, the king cried "Have at you!" (which is what men used to cry when they started to fight) and he and Pellinore spurred their horses and came together with all their might. Their long spears met on their shields and were shattered to pieces. Up rode their attendants with fresh spears and again they rode furiously at one another, and the crash of their spears on the metal shields set all the leaves of the forest quivering.

'They sprang from their horses, and drew their swords, and after a few moments of desperate fighting, the stranger knight brought his sword down upon Arthur's sword with such force that he broke the king's weapon in two pieces, and Arthur was left defenceless. Then they fought with their bare hands and Pellinore threw King

Arthur to the ground and pulled off his helmet and would
have killed him, but Merlin, who was watching, stepped
forward, for he could not allow the king to die in his
youth. He wove a magic spell around the stranger knight,
which threw him into a deep sleep, and then he turned to
Arthur and said:

' "Sire, your sword is broken and you can fight no
more till you have another. Come with me and I will show
you where you may find one."

'So they rode till they came to a lake, which was a fair
water and broad, and in the middle of the lake Arthur saw
an arm, clothed in white samite – that's a kind of silk
stuff. In the hand was a sword. On the hilt gleamed
jewels, and the blade of it flashed in the sun. The king
stood motionless, gazing at this strange sight, and as he
watched, he saw a maiden approaching him across the
water.'

'*Walking* on the water?' asked Sue.

'Walking on it,' answered the dragon, 'just as easily
as you or I tread the grass of a meadow or the sand on
the seashore.

' "She is the Lady of the Lake," said Merlin to Arthur,
in a low voice. "Ask her courteously how you may get
the sword."

'So Arthur said: "Lady of the Lake, what sword is
that, which the arm is holding above the water? I would
it were mine, for I have no sword."

'The Lady of the Lake led Arthur a little way along
the water's edge and showed him a barge, lying hidden
among the reeds. She told him to get into it and row towards the middle of the lake and take the sword from the
mysterious hand.

'So Merlin and the king tied their horses to two trees and they rowed across the smooth water and as they approached they could see that the hand that held the sword was small and fine and white, and was the hand of a woman. Gently Arthur took the sword from its clasp, and as soon as he held it in his own hand, the arm, in its sleeve of white samite, disappeared beneath the water. Merlin had read of this sword in one of his magic books, when he was studying in his house with the seventy windows and the sixty doors, and he told Arthur that the sword was called Excalibur, and that as long as he wore it he would never be defeated in battle.'

'And did he always wear it?' asked Sue.

'Always,' answered the dragon, 'and he won many victories with it, but in the end, as you shall hear one of these days, the sword was given back to the Lady of the Lake.'

'Where's the lake?' asked Susan. 'In Cornwall?'

'Yes, it's in Cornwall. Not so very far from Tintagel, in the heart of Bodmin Moor.'

'How mysterious it sounds, Bodmin Moor,' said Susan, slowly. 'It sounds purple and black and secret. I suppose –'

She stopped, and the dragon gazed thoughtfully at her.

'I know. You want to go there,' he said, kindly. 'I'll make you a promise. I'll take you there as a good-bye present, if the magic goes on working that long. Will that make up for not having gone anywhere today?'

'Oh, yes, yes!' cried Susan. 'You are a darling dragon! Now shall we have our picnic?'

The dragon rose to his feet.

'I will invite you to come into my cave to eat it,' he said, solemnly.

Susan felt very honoured. She picked up the picnic basket and followed the dragon into the cave. The cave went a very long way back into the cliffs. It was high and arched overhead like a church, and the bare rock glistened with water.

'Isn't it awfully wet in here?' asked Susan.

'It doesn't worry me,' said the dragon. 'My scales are damp-proof.'

'Like macintosh?'

'I expect so. Isn't macintosh that stuff you humans wear in the rain?'

'Yes,' answered Sue. 'I've got a macintosh hat, *and* rubber boots, too.'

'It's more convenient to have scales growing on you,' said the dragon in a superior voice, and led the way deeper into the cave.

It was quite dark now and the opening was only a small yellow patch behind them. Susan could see well enough, as the dragon's lamp-like eyes acted as torches, and shed beams of light wherever he looked.

'We'll sit here,' he said at last, and pointed to a convenient shelf of rock.

'This is actually my bed,' he went on. 'I have several rugs. Wait a moment, I'll get one out for you to sit on.'

The dragon reached up into a kind of cupboard in the rock, and produced a large, dark-brown rug, neatly folded. When he had spread it out, Susan saw that it was made of seaweed, tightly woven together.

'Did you *make* it?' she asked, admiringly.

'Well, no,' answered the dragon, reluctantly. 'A lady friend of mine made it. A mermaid.'

'You do have lovely friends,' sighed Susan.

'So do you,' retorted the dragon. 'You have me.' He smiled a very amiable smile at her, and pulled a bag out of the picnic basket.

'Now what have we here?' he said. 'Ah, a bun. Only one bun?'

'We're to share it.'

'All right. Wait a minute,' said the dragon. 'We must have knives and plates and do the thing in style.'

He reached up to another shelf-like piece of rock, and took down two stone plates, and a thin blade made of a seashell (the kind called a razor-blade) with which he elegantly cut the cake in half. He put a half bun on each plate, and then opened the second bag.

'Ah!' he said, his eyes gleaming with satisfaction. '*Two* chocolate biscuits. One each.'

He laid them on the plates.

'We'll see to the banana afterwards,' he said. 'One of us might be too full to want his half, and then, of course, the other might eat it all, just to save wasting it, don't you think?'

'Well,' answered Sue, rather doubtfully. She liked bananas.

They ate their pieces of bun and the chocolate biscuits, and then the dragon produced two big, curly seashells, like goblets, and they drank the orangeade to the last drop.

'Your very good health!' cried the dragon, as he raised his shell to his mouth.

'And yours!' cried Susan. The orangeade had never tasted nicer. The shells were rather salty with sea-water and somehow that improved the flavour of the drink and made it taste slightly magical.

'Now, about the banana,' began the dragon. 'Shall I cut it in half or don't you want half?'

'Well,' said Susan. 'I'd like a *piece*. Perhaps not quite half.'

'All right,' said the dragon, graciously. 'Here we go.'

He really cut the banana quite fairly, giving himself a piece only a very little bigger than Sue's, and, after all, Sue said to herself, he was a much larger creature than she was and must feel much hungrier.

'Lovely,' said the dragon, at last. 'Quite lovely. I *have* enjoyed that.'

'So have I,' answered Susan.

The dragon took a green handkerchief out of a box on a shelf just above his bed, and wiped his claws carefully with it, and mopped his lips.

'There! That's better,' he said. 'Want to borrow it?'

'Oh, thank you,' said Sue. The green handkerchief was rather damp and seaweedy but she didn't like to refuse, and it certainly was very pretty. In one corner the dragon's initials – R.D. – were embroidered in cowrie shells.

'Tell me about your mermaid,' said Sue.

The dragon thought for a moment. Then he said, unexpectedly: 'Shall we go and see her?'

'Oh, dragon, what a wonderful idea! But I thought you said you were too tired today.'

'I feel better now after my picnic," said the dragon. 'Look, I tell you what. Let me have a little nap. You go back to your mother and have your lunch and after lunch come here again, and I'll take you over to Kynance Cove to meet the mermaid. Mind you, I can't promise that she'll come out and speak to you. She's shy and she doesn't like humans any more than I do. But if I tell her you're harmless, she *might* come.'

'You won't forget, will you?' asked Sue, anxiously.

''Course not!' cried the dragon. 'Anyway, this will remind me.'

He lashed his tail round, sending up a shower of sand, and as Susan watched, she saw, to her great astonishment, that the long green tail was tied in a knot.

'Why!' she cried, 'That's what Mummy does when she wants to remember something. Only, of course, she ties it in her handkerchief, not in her tail.'

'A tail is far better,' said the dragon. 'You can lose a handkerchief, but you can't lose a tail.'

He laughed heartily at his own joke, and waved his knotted tail gaily to and fro.

'Goodness!' cried Sue. 'Don't lose your tail. You would look funny – not a bit like a dragon. But I expect I'd love you just as much.'

'That's a comfort to me,' said the dragon.

So, in great excitement, Sue packed the paper bags and the orangeade bottle into the picnic basket, and washed the plates and the shell goblets in a rock pool, and ran off down the cave into the open sunshine, leaving the dragon settled down on his rug for a nap, with his knotted tail tucked round him.

CHAPTER SIX

The Mermaid with a Comb in Her Hair

In the afternoon, when Sue went down to the cave, she could hear a voice, a rather high, reedy voice, singing a nursery rhyme, but the words were quite different from those Sue knew herself. She did not like to call out, so she listened and this is what she heard, sung to the tune of 'Oranges and Lemons', in the dragon's tuneful but rather thin, quavering voice:

'Three naked lads
Say the bells of St Chad's;
Three silver pickles
Say the bells of St Michael's;
Three golden canaries
Say the bells of St Mary's;
Black pots and pans
Say the bells of St Bran's.'

Sue called softly to the dragon when the song was over.

He came out, humming the tune gaily and waving his tail in time to it.

'I know that song,' said Susan. 'At least, I know the tune of it, but my words are quite different.'

'And what are your words?' asked the dragon with kindly interest, sitting down in a listening attitude.

> *'Oranges and lemons,*
> *Say the bells of St Clement's;*
> *You owe me five farthings,*
> *Say the bells of St Martin's;*
> *When will you pay me?*
> *Say the bells of Old Bailey;*
> *When I grow rich,*
> *Say the bells of Shoreditch;*
> *When will that be?*
> *Say the bells of Stepney;*
> *I do not know,*
> *Says the great bell of Bow.'*

'Very nice,' said the dragon. 'I'm afraid I don't know any of those places.'

'I think they are all in London,' said Sue.

'I've never been to London and never want to,' said the dragon, firmly. 'I have heard that it is dirty, foggy, noisy, smelly and damp.'

Susan loved London, but after this she didn't like to say anything more about it, so she asked the dragon where *his* song came from.

'From the borders of Wales,' he answered. 'I heard it once when I was travelling in those parts. Can't remember when, or where exactly.'

'Talking about remembering,' said Sue, hopefully, 'you – you haven't forgotten, have you?'

'Forgotten what?' asked the dragon, lifting his eyebrows very high indeed.

'Well, forgotten what you said we might do this afternoon?'

'I wonder what it could have been?' said the dragon, scratching one ear with maddening calm. 'You see, until I remember what it was that we said we might do, I can't tell whether I've forgotten it or not.'

'Oh, do please remember!' cried Sue, in an agonized voice. 'You tied a knot in your tail to remind you.'

The dragon gazed sadly at the knot.

'Ah,' he sighed. 'I can see the knot clearly enough, but what was it *for*? Would it have been something to do with magic?'

'Yes, oh, yes!'

The dragon began to hum, and turning his back on Susan, began rubbing the claws of one paw against the soft pads of the other, as Susan had seen her father do, when he wanted to polish up his nails. The dragon's humming turned into an actual song, and he rubbed his claws energetically in time to the rollicking tune, swaying slightly from side to side:

> *One Friday morn, when we set sail,*
>   *And our ship not far from land,*
> *We there espied a fair, pretty maid,*
>   *With a comb and a glass in her hand, her hand, her hand,*
>   *With a comb and a glass in her hand.'*

The dragon turned round suddenly.

'That's a song the sailors used to sing about a mer-

maid,' he said. 'Rather a jolly tune, I always thought.'

'A mermaid?' breathed Sue. 'Then we *are* going –'

The dragon interrupted her.

'I must tidy up,' he said. 'Clean my claws and comb my hair.'

'Your hair?' asked Susan, looking doubtfully at the dragon's scaly hide. 'I don't see any hair.'

'Between my ears,' said the dragon, 'I have some very pleasing hair, thick and curly. I found a bottle of hair restorer, once, left behind by some careless tripper, and rubbed it on my head. There wasn't very much of it, unfortunately, only enough to rub into the patch between my ears, but it grew the hair all right. I'm surprised you haven't noticed it.'

'You're rather tall,' said Susan. 'I've never seen on top of your head before. Oh, what a lovely comb!'

The dragon was gently drawing through his curls a large ivory comb, the handle of which was studded with shells of glowing colours. She reached out for it, but the dragon whisked it away.

'Oh, mayn't I see it, dragon?'

'Well, you can look at it,' said the dragon, holding it towards her rather unwillingly, 'but I'd rather you didn't hold it. You might break it.'

'Is it very precious?'

'Very. It was given to me by the mermaid.'

'A *real* mermaid?'

'My dear child,' said the dragon severely. 'Either a person is real, or he isn't there at all. I don't talk about you as a *real* Susan. Of course she is a real mermaid. I have known her for centuries, though I don't often see her now. I first found her sitting on a rock, arranging her hair in the mirror of a small clear pool. As soon as I appeared, she slipped off the rock and hid beneath the water. I could see she was afraid of me – such a pity all these maidens were afraid of me.'

'You used to eat them,' Sue reminded him.

'Well, well, that was long ago,' said the dragon, and sighing, he licked his lips. 'Some of them tasted nice, you know,' he added regretfully.

'If you did that in front of her – licking your lips, I mean – I'm not surprised the mermaid hid in the water.'

'Now, now,' said the dragon, drawing himself up. 'Don't get ideas into your head. I'm a good dragon now, aren't I?'

Sue feared that he must have forgotten again about the promise, but she did not like to remind him. She thought that perhaps he was better employed telling her a story than licking his lips, which made him look rather fierce, so she hastily agreed that he was, of course, a good dragon now, and she begged him to go on with the story.

'Well, once I was strolling along the cliffs, above Kynance Cove. It was a fine morning, a long, long time ago. No one about. The sea as blue as blue. Suddenly I saw a fair-haired creature – an ordinary woman I thought it was – sitting on a rock in the cove beneath me. She was combing out her yellow hair, and it hung round her like a tent. She was using the pool as a mirror, leaning over it, with her comb in her hand, and very beautiful she looked. I slipped down the cliff path and came up behind her and wished her a polite "Good morning!" You should have seen her jump! Her yellow hair rose up around her like seaweed in a pool. I saw her silver gleaming tail then, and I knew she was a mermaid.

'"Now, my dear," said I, "I won't hurt you. I'm not a human being. I'm a friendly, well-disposed dragon. You've no need to be afraid." She wouldn't answer me at first, but at last I coaxed her into telling me how she'd come ashore with her husband and children, earlier in the morning, at midtide. The merman fell asleep on some soft green weed in a cave, out of the sunlight, and the little ones played on the sands, in and out of the waves. The mermaid herself had floated idly about from pool to pool, diving down to pick sprays of seaweed which she had made into a bunch to take home with her. Suddenly, as she was telling me this, she looked round towards the sea. The tide was right out and the sea was far away.

'"Oh, the sea! the sea!" she cried, and burst into tears. "It's gone! What shall I do? What shall I do?"

'I tried to comfort her in my dragonish way. I told her

that if only she would wait for a few more hours, the tide would come in again and float her out to sea, but she set up a terrible crying.

'"My husband!" she wailed. "It will soon be time for his dinner, and I not there to get it for him."

'"Let him get it for himself," said I. "No one gets my dinner for me."

'"Ah," she sighed. "You don't understand. You're such a gentle creature, I don't believe you would ever harm anyone but my husband is not like you. Why, if he were hungry, he would eat one of our children as soon as look at it. Oh, help me down to the sea, dragon, do please help me to the sea, and I will give you a gift – only help me!"

'Well, of course I said I would help her. I knelt down on the sand and she climbed on to my back and clasped her arms round my neck. I could feel her cold, finny fingers on my throat. Off we went to the sea. When we reached the edge of the waves, she slipped off my back and into the foam like a fish, and then she lay in the shallow water and called to me:

'"Thank you a thousand times, dragon. Here is my comb (and she took this very comb out of her long golden hair and tossed it towards me). If ever I can help you, or give you a wish, comb the water with it, and I will come to you and grant you your wish." '

'And have you ever combed the water?' asked Sue.

'Oh, yes,' said the dragon. 'Several times, when I've wanted some little thing, like these rugs, for instance, or a couple of handkerchiefs, or a toothbrush. The mermaid makes them all for me; she's an obliging creature.'

'Were we – were we going to see her?' asked Sue, rather hesitatingly.

'See her?' exclaimed the dragon in tones of the utmost surprise, as if the idea had never occurred to him.

'You did actually *promise*,' said Susan.

'Now, I wonder *when* I promised,' mused the dragon. 'Was it last Wednesday?'

'No,' said Susan.

'Was it – a year ago, last Midsummer Day?'

'No, no! I wasn't even here then,' cried Susan.

'It wouldn't have been about fifty years ago, would it?' asked the dragon, looking at Susan very solemnly.

'No, of course not. I wasn't born,' exclaimed Susan, in an agony of impatience at the dragon's forgetfulness.

'Then it must have been this morning,' he said at last, with an air of triumph.

'Of course it was this morning. I keep telling you – you tied a knot in your tail. How *can* you have forgotten? Or were you teasing?'

'Perhaps I was,' said the dragon, his yellow eyes glinting. 'Never mind. I've remembered for good now, so I can undo the knot.'

He turned round and untied the knot in his tail.

'Now, get on my back, and we'll see if we can get to Kynance Cove. But I'm not making any promises about seeing the mermaid, much less talking to her. She's very shy. Maybe she won't even come out of the sea.'

'Oh, I do hope she does!' cried Susan, as she climbed on to the dragon's back.

Once again, she clung on to his scaly back, and his skin, warmed by the sun, felt just like the leather of the car seats, only it smelt different – a salty, seaweedy smell, like rocks at low tide.

'Now,' said the dragon, gathering himself together rather like a cat that is about to spring at your mother's ball of wool, 'NOW – I'm for Kynance Cove!'

'I'm for Kynance Cove!' shouted Susan. 'I'm for Kynance Cove!'

This time, the dragon soared into the air straight away, and to Susan's alarm headed out to sea.

'Dragon, dragon, where *are* we going?' she cried into his windswept ears.

'It's all right,' the dragon called back. 'Don't be frightened. I didn't want to go over the beach and the cliffs. Too many people. If I sail out to sea for a bit they'll think I'm a new kind of helicopter, and then we can go inland further down the coast, where there aren't so many people.'

'But I might slip off,' wailed Susan, 'and I should hate to fall into the sea.'

'It's softer than falling on to the land,' observed the dragon.

'But I might drown!'

'Not with me here, you wouldn't. I'd never let you. I'd rescue you in a trice,' said the dragon and Sue felt rather more comfortable. After all, he was a very wonderful dragon.

They were soon back over the land, and sailing along quite fast. The fields and roads lay spread out below them. Sue could see cars scurrying along like beetles, and sometimes there was a puff of smoke, and a thin, snake-like creature could be seen running along through the fields. It took her several minutes to realize that it was a train.

Cornwall is a long, thin county, and it doesn't take long to get from one side of it to the other. Kynance Cove was on the opposite side to Constantine Bay and Sue had never been over to this part of Cornwall before. It looked rockier, and the coves were smaller than the ones round Constantine Bay. In fact, seen from above, the coast looked as if someone had gone along it taking very small neat round bites out of it, with his sharp teeth.

'There's Kynance!' cried the dragon, suddenly, braking so sharply that Susan slid forward. He pointed down to one of the coves and added:

'Goodness! there seem to be rather a lot of people there.'

'It's not so bad up in the corner,' said Sue. 'Over there! Look, there doesn't seem to be anyone that side at all.'

'Good,' said the dragon. 'That's the side of the cove that the mermaid likes best. It's full of rocky pools and the water is deeper.'

They began to sweep downwards over the cliffs. Sue could feel her ears humming and tingling, as they do sometimes when you go downhill in a car. The dragon landed on a convenient ledge of cliff, just above the rocky end of the cove. There was no one about, except a gull who flew away squawking. It was a foolish, ignorant creature and had never seen a dragon before.

'I'll just have ten minutes' nap,' said the dragon, and, closing his eyes firmly, he lay back in a grassy hollow, and crossed his back legs.

Sue looked about her. The ledge they were on was not frightening, as the cliff sloped down towards the sea in a number of step-like ledges. It was easy to climb down on

to the next one, and then on to the next, and this she did, till she reached the rocks. The pools were green and cold, and so clear that she could see the tiny shells lying on the bottom, the dark-red anemones, and little scuttling crabs, which ran busily hither and thither, while from side to side of the pools swam shoals of minute fish, darting so quickly through the water that they looked like flashes of light.

The sea was calm and splashed gently against the far rocks, only occasionally sending up a light cloud of spray when some really big wave came rolling in.

Sitting on the edge of the rocks, waiting for the dragon to finish his forty winks, Susan trailed seaweed in the clear water and watched it spread out like a flower, and sang softly to herself:

> '*I had a little nut tree, nothing would it bear*
> *But a silver nutmeg and a golden pear;*
> *The King of Spain's daughter came to visit me,*
> *And all for the sake of my little nut tree.*
> *I skipped over water, I danced over sea,*
> *And all the birds in the air couldn't catch me.*'

Sue was particularly fond of this song, and she sang the last two lines again, swirling the seaweed in and out of the water in time to the music:

> '*I skipped over water, I danced over sea,*
> *And all the birds in the air couldn't catch me.*'

As she stopped singing, she heard a strange sound, a kind of humming, high and clear and watery, rising from the sea, as it washed round the rocks. Thinking for a moment that it was the wind, Sue took no notice, but then it seemed to her that it was a definite tune, and that it was coming from the water just below her. This was very deep and in shadow. She could not see far down into it, but as she listened, the music became quite clear. It was someone singing, and the words were:

> *'I have a deep-sea garden, nothing will it grow*
> *But cowries and coral and sea-mistletoe.*
> *A sailor came swimming down through the foam,*
> *And all to visit my deep-sea home.*
> *I plucked him pink coral, I gave him a shell,*
> *But who had given him the gifts he never could tell.'*

'I know! I know!' called Sue, leaning down over the sea with her face as close to the water as she dared. 'I know who you are. You're a mermaid. You're a friend of my dragon, of R. *Dragon*,' she added, thinking that the mermaid might know several dragons. 'Please come out, mermaid, because I'm a friend of R. Dragon's as well.'

The calm, smooth surface of the sea rippled slightly and the singing ceased.

'Please come, dear mermaid,' called Sue softly, and drew her seaweed over the water. There was a long silence.

'Don't go away,' pleaded Sue. 'Oh, I do wish dragon would come. He'd comb the water with his magic comb, and then you'd have to come.'

Pretending her seaweed was a comb, Sue drew it quickly over the water several times. There was a sudden rippling and the green water heaved into folds, as though someone were pushing it aside like a curtain, and there appeared, close to the rock on which she was sitting, the golden hair and startled eyes of a mermaid. The mermaid and Sue looked at each other for a few moments without speaking.

'You're a human child,' said the mermaid, at last. 'But you sang what sounded like my song.'

'You sang *mine*,' said Sue, 'only it had different words. Oh, you *are* beautiful!'

'Are you alone?' asked the mermaid.

'Except for dragon,' said Sue. 'R. Dragon. He's having a nap.'

The mermaid smiled suddenly.

'How like him,' she said. 'When he wakes up he'll be hungry. I'd better pop down and get him a slice of seaweed cake or a deep-sea bun.'

'Why, do *you* give him buns, too?' asked Sue. 'I'm always having to give him mine. He seems terribly fond of them.'

The mermaid laughed out loud at this, a trickling laugh like water splashing over a rock.

'You're a friend of his, are you?' she said. 'I'm so glad he's got a friend. I've always been afraid that he might be lonely these days. Are you very fond of him?'

'Oh, very,' said Sue. 'He's the most wonderful person I've ever known – except you, of course,' she added hastily.

'Thank you. That's a polite thing to say,' said the mermaid. 'But a dragon *is* a most wonderful creature. I've always thought so, and I've seen whales and sea monsters and sea serpents, too. Tell me how you got here.'

'We flew,' answered Susan.

The mermaid nodded her head as if she were not at all surprised at this. Then she reached up her arm, and touched Susan's cheek. Her skin was covered with tiny silver scales, like a fish, and the touch of her hand was ice cold, but pleasant, like the salty tang of sea-water.

'You're just a little girl,' she said. 'How old are you?'

'Eight,' answered Susan. 'How old are your children?'

'Oh, they've all grown up and left me,' said the mermaid, sadly. 'Years and years ago. They're all married and have had children and grandchildren and great grandchildren now.'

'But –' Sue looked at her fresh, silvery face, and the golden hair that floated round her shoulders. 'But *you* don't look old.'

'Mermaids grow up, but they never grow old,' she explained. 'I suppose you've never met a mermaid before?'

'Never.'

'In the old days, we did sometimes show ourselves to humans and speak with them, but then they grew foolish and wrote books about us, trying to make out that we were really nothing but fish, so we kept out of their way after that. Otherwise they might have caught us in their nets and sent us to the fishmongers' shops. You don't think I'm like a fish, do you?'

'No, of course not,' said Sue at once. 'But I would like to see your tail all the same.'

'You shall,' said the mermaid, laughing.

There was a flash of silver, and there she was sitting on the rock beside Susan, and her silver body ended in a tail, forked like a fish and shiny with scales.

'What's your name, mermaid?' asked Susan, gazing at her with wide-open eyes.

At once the mermaid drew away from her.

'I would never tell you that,' she said.

'I think I know why,' said Sue, remembering something the dragon had told her. 'You're like the fairies and the dragons. You can't give your name to people or they'd have power over you.'

'Yes, that's quite right,' agreed the mermaid. 'But I'm sorry, because I like you, and perhaps you wouldn't have used the power. All the same, I must keep to the rule. It would never do to break it. A mermaid I knew once told her name to a sailor, and he gained such power over her foolish heart that she left the sea and went to live among mortals.'

'But could she *walk*?'

'Ah, no, she couldn't. That was just the trouble. Once they'd got her, they put her in a tank and then the sailor took her round to all the circuses and fairs and showed her off to people at sixpence a time. Thousands came to see her, and the sailor grew richer and richer, but the mermaid pined away.'

'How horrid!' exclaimed Sue. 'He didn't deserve to grow rich.'

'Well, he didn't stay rich. After the mermaid had pined away, he wasted all his money, and then he would spend hours down by the shore trying to get another mermaid into his clutches, but we all knew him, and none of us would come when he whistled and called to us. He grew thin and old, and at last, one night, a high wind rose, and the waves grew restless, and caught him as he stood on the shore, and carried him away to sea.'

'Then I won't even try to find out your name,' said Sue. 'I'll just be glad I can see you. Like the dragon. I don't know what the R. stands for, do you?'

'Oh, yes, I do,' answered the mermaid, mysteriously. 'And that reminds me. I ought to go and get his bun. You run and wake him up.'

'All right,' said Sue, and scrambled up over the rocks, while the mermaid disappeared into the sea.

The dragon was still asleep when Sue clambered up on to his ledge. His mouth was open and he was snoring gently. Every time he snored, a little puff of green smoke popped out of his nostrils. Sue tickled his ears with a piece of dry seaweed and he twitched without opening his eyes.

'Dragon! R. Dragon!' called Sue, softly, not wanting to startle him.

'Kerchoo!' sneezed the dragon, as Susan ran the sea-weed over his nose. 'Kerchoo-oo-oo!' and the green smoke went up in a cloud into the air, just as it had the very first day that Sue met the dragon, and he had sneezed in the cave.

'Wake up!' cried Sue, tickling him again.

The dragon opened his eyes.

'Were you tickling me?' he asked, suspiciously.

'Only a little,' confessed Sue.

'I wasn't asleep,' said the dragon at once.

'Oh, dragon, you *were*!'

'Wasn't,' said the dragon, who, like most of us, felt cross when he first woke up. 'Anyway,' he added (trying to change the subject), 'where are we?'

'At Kynance Cove,' answered Susan.

'Goodness!' said the dragon. 'However did we get here? We'd better be getting back home at once. I didn't realize we'd come so far.'

'But, dragon, we came here to see the mermaid.'

'No time,' said the dragon, scratching at his tickly ear with a claw. 'No time.'

Sue almost cried with vexation. What a very tiresome creature the dragon could be, she thought.

'Dragon, please, *please* wake up properly and remember.'

'Remember what? How can I remember something I've forgotten?' said the dragon, scowling.

Susan had a bright idea.

'Would it make you feel better if you had a bun, dear dragon?'

'You haven't got one,' said the dragon, gloomily. 'Your mother doesn't give you one in the afternoon, I don't suppose.'

'But I know where there is one,' said Sue. 'It's – it's a kind of magic.'

'You can't do magic,' said the dragon.

'But I've met someone who can, and there's a bun waiting for you.'

The dragon began to mutter to himself: 'She knows someone who can do magic. Now who can she have met?

I don't suppose she'll want her old dragon any more.
She'll be leaving me for her new friends. They can
probably do better magic than me. Nasty aeroplanes, I
shouldn't wonder, or helicopters.'

Susan caught hold of the dragon's left ear and gave it a
pull.

'You're a silly old dragon,' she said. 'And you're
horribly forgetful – worse than Mummy. *Do* come
on.'

The dragon followed her down the sloping cliff edge
till they reached the rocks. Lying on a flat slab of clean
rock were three buns and three slices of cake. There was
no one to be seen. Sue looked round for the mermaid, but
there was not a sign of her.

The dragon stopped dead and stared at the buns and
slices of cake.

'What's that?' he said, in surprised tones.

'It *looks* like three buns and three bits of cake,' said
Sue, hardly able to stop herself from laughing.

The dragon took a few steps forward and sniffed suspiciously at the food. Then he looked round at Susan:

'D'you know anything about this?' he asked.

''Course I do!'

'Is it good to eat?'

''Course it is!'

'Then let's eat it,' said the dragon, and picked up the
largest bun, which was *not* the one nearest to him.

There was a kind of bubbling in the water below the
rock, that sounded very like someone laughing. The
dragon paused, with his bun half-way to his mouth.

'What's that?' he said.

Bubble, bubble, went the water.

'Where did you say we were?' asked the dragon, rubbing his eyes which were still full of sleep.

'Kynance Cove.'

'But that's where the mermaid lives!' cried the dragon. 'Whyever didn't you tell me before?'

'I did! I did! and you wouldn't take any notice.'

'Silly old me,' said the dragon, smiling a wide smile. 'Do you see that bubbling down there? That's her laughing.'

'Is it really?' said Sue.

'Sure to be. And I wouldn't be surprised if she put – what did you say just now about meeting someone who could do magic? Don't tell me you've met the mermaid already?'

'I have! I have!' shrieked Sue. 'We've had a long talk, and she put buns and cake out for us and –'

'And here she is,' said the mermaid, rising from the water like a silver fish.

The dragon was delighted at the joke that had been played upon him. He rolled about with laughing, choked

on a crumb of cake, and had to be patted severely on his scaly back by Susan. Then they sat in the sunshine, eating the rest of the tea, and the dragon told the mermaid how he had met Sue and the mermaid told the dragon how *she* had met Sue and they were all very pleased with themselves.

'What's it like under the sea?' asked Susan, at last, when they were sitting back on the rocks, wiping the crumbs off their fingers and paws.

'It's very strange and beautiful,' said the mermaid. 'The floor is of fine sand. You would think you were walking on gold. There are black, gleaming rocks, as high as mountains, and great sea-weeds as tall as trees, that wave their branches in the moving water, as your forests do in the wind. Far out under the sea lies a city, with houses and streets and churches and palaces. That's where some of us mer-people have our homes. We live in the drowned houses and sleep on soft beds, where once mortal people slept. We eat off tables, and use the cups and plates and knives and forks of the mortals.'

Sue looked at the mermaid, round-eyed.

'But how did the city get there?' she asked.

'Once it was dry land,' said the mermaid. 'The land of Lyonesse. But one night a terrible storm arose. The waves grew higher and higher and rolled up the beaches and over the cliffs. The land of Lyonesse sank beneath the waves. On stormy nights, the bells in the churches are set ringing by the waves, and the Cornish people say you can hear them, tolling in the deeps of the sea. But to us mer-people living on the sea-bed, storms make no difference. The waves may rock the bells at the top of the church steeples, but we live in the green, still waters below. We swim in and out of the open doors of the houses, and our mer-babies play in the gardens, where flowers of the sea grow now, instead of sweet williams and stocks and chrysanthemums.'

'I wish I could go there,' sighed Sue. 'I suppose you've been, dragon?'

'Many times,' answered the dragon. 'I am an old family friend. I am invited for weeks at a time, though I don't go so often now. It's a bit far for me.'

The mermaid took Sue's hand in her own silvery one.

'One day,' she said, 'you must come and visit me again. I will ask the mer-king if he will permit you to enter our kingdom, and if he will, we will say a charm over you which will give you power to breathe and live under the sea, and you shall visit us, and stay in my house in the drowned city of Lyonesse.'

'Oh, thank you!' cried Sue. 'You are a dear mermaid. I shall never forget meeting you.'

Sue looked from the mermaid to the dragon and then back again to the mermaid.

'Except for my mother and father,' she said, 'and my cat, Pooker, I don't think anybody in the whole world is as nice as you and dragon.'

'Hooray for us!' cried the dragon.

The mermaid smiled at Sue.

'I must go back now,' she said. 'We must say good-bye. But one day, you will come and visit me again, won't you?'

'Shall I sing that song about the King of Spain's daughter, if I want you?'

'Yes, sing that one. If ever I hear you singing it, I'll come. But it might be a long, long time before we meet again, and I don't want to forget you. Will you give me something?'

Sue thought hard.

'I've not got very much I *can* give you, except my handkerchief, and that's rather grubby.'

'Would you give me that pretty thing in your hair?'

'My clip?' asked Sue. It was a blue one shaped like a bird. 'Of course I'll give it to you.'

She undid it and gave it to the mermaid who turned it over and over in her silver hand and admired it. Then she looked up at Sue.

'I'll give you something in return,' she said. 'To remember *me* by.'

She took a tiny ring off her little finger. It was quite different from any ring Susan had ever seen, for it was a silver fish, curled into a circle, and biting its own tail. Sue slipped it on her middle finger and it just fitted.

'Now, good-bye!' called the mermaid.

'Good-bye! Good-bye and thank you!' cried Susan. 'Thank you, dear mermaid.'

'Good-bye,' said the dragon, and reached out his paw. He took the mermaid's hand and kissed it politely. Then the mermaid waved to them and with a flash of silver, slipped beneath the water.

Susan didn't talk at all to the dragon on her way home. She had so much to think about and to remember. Only, just as they were landing at Constantine Bay, she said:

'Don't you *love* the mermaid, dragon?'

'Very much,' he answered.

'Have you known her a very long time?'

'Several hundred years. If she'd been a dragon, or if I'd been a merman, I might have married her.'

'Would you marry me,' asked Susan, 'if I was grown-up and a dragon, I mean?'

The dragon looked at Susan out of the corner of his eyes.

'Perhaps,' he said. 'But I'm not really a marrying dragon. I'm a crusty old bachelor, and better off by myself in my cave.'

'But you are happy, aren't you, dear dragon?' asked Sue, anxiously.

'Yes, thank you,' answered the dragon. 'I've a nice cave for my home, and two good friends, and I can still do magic, and blow green smoke out of my nose, and what more can a dragon want?'

'All right,' said Sue. 'I won't worry about you any more, only sometimes I have wondered if you weren't lonely.'

'You're a kind, thoughtful child,' said the dragon, and blew her a green kiss.

Susan ran across the sand and climbed over the rocks, and in a few minutes she found her father and mother who were lying and sun-bathing, just as they had been when she had left them, it seemed, several hours before. She flung herself down beside them, and held up her ring.

'Look what I've got!' she cried.

'Hullo,' said her father. 'Where did you get that?'

'A mermaid gave it to me,' said Susan.

'I thought it was a dragon you were friends with,' said her mother. 'Don't tell me he's changed into a mermaid.'

'Oh, no,' said Susan. 'But he took me to see her. She was beautiful and she gave me this as a – as a –'

'As a keepsake?'

'Yes. And d'you know what I gave her?'

'What, darling?'

'My blue bird clip. She asked for it.'

'Oh, so that's why your hair is looking so untidy,' said Sue's mother, with a sigh. 'We shall have to get you another, I suppose. You are a terrible child the way you lose your clips.'

'I didn't lose this one. I gave it away.'

'Perhaps you did, but it's gone just the same. Well, let's put your bathing cap on and we'll all have a bathe.'

So that day ended in a glorious swim, and as Sue splashed about in the shallow water, she remembered the mermaid and the drowned city of Lyonesse, and how the mer-people swam in and out of the open doors of the houses.

'One day,' she said to herself. 'One day, when I'm bigger and can swim properly, I'll go there.'

CHAPTER SEVEN

How to Get the Better of a Giant

N EXT day Sue found the dragon in a very good humour.
He was sweeping out his cave with a broom made of dried
seaweed, and singing to himself as he worked, to the tune
of 'Old MacDougall had a Farm':

> *'Old R. Dragon had a cave*
> *Down in Constantine-O!*
> *And in that cave there was some dust –*
> *With a brush-brush here*
> *And a sweep-sweep there!*
> *Here a sweep, there a sweep,*
> *Here and there a brush-brush!'*

He was wearing a green apron with yellow spots.
'Did the mermaid make that for you?' asked Sue.
'She did,' answered the dragon, as he took the apron
off carefully, shook it and folded it up before putting it
away on a rock shelf. 'It was a Christmas present to me
years ago.'

'Goodness, it's lasted well,' exclaimed Susan.

'Oh, things that mermaids make don't wear out for centuries,' said the dragon. 'Look at this handkerchief.'

He took an old cigar box down from a shelf, and opened it and took out a handkerchief. It was the same one that Susan had seen when she had the picnic with the dragon in the cave, a bright green handkerchief with R.D. embroidered in cowries in one corner.

'She made me a set of six of these, exactly a hundred years ago come Michaelmas. For my birthday. I lost one in the sea, but I've still got the other five and as good as new.'

'They're very pretty,' said Sue. 'I wish I knew what the R. stood for.'

'Perhaps you will one day,' said the dragon, kindly.

'I did like it when you kissed her hand,' said Susan. 'It looked so polite. I've never seen anyone do that before.'

'Never seen anyone?' The dragon looked surprised. 'Doesn't your father kiss the hands of ladies he greets?'

'I never saw him do it,' said Sue.

'It's a sad world,' observed the dragon, with a sigh.

'I think it must have changed rather since you were young.'

'People were taught manners in my youth,' said the dragon. 'Manners first, spelling and sums afterwards. As I told you, I learnt mine at the court of King Arthur. Ah, what a court it was!'

The dragon leaned on his seaweed broom and gazed across the empty sands with a faraway look in his eyes.

'I remember when Arthur married Guinevere. The rejoicings at that wedding were something I've never seen the like of before or since. A hundred musicians were there, twanging away at their harps, blowing trumpets, and singing songs, and such dancing, and merry-making, and, of course, food by the wagon-load. Two or three of us dragons buried enough of it to last a twelvemonth.'

'Oh,' said Susan. 'Do you bury food – like dogs?'

'Not at all like dogs,' answered the dragon, looking most offended. 'We bury it like dragons.'

'Does it keep nice?' asked Susan doubtfully.

'Very nice indeed. In fact, it improves,' answered the dragon, licking his lips. 'I have a couple of geese, three turkeys, and seventeen hens buried – well, I won't tell you *where* they are buried – but, anyway, buried safely for my Christmas dinner.'

'Wherever did you find them?' asked Susan, staring at the dragon.

'Oh, well.' The dragon coughed a little cough. 'Well, let's say I just picked them up here and there.'

Susan thought privately that he must have stolen them from neighbouring farms, but she did not like to say so, and thought it better to change the subject.

'It's lovely and cool in here, and terribly hot outside,' she began. 'Could we stay in here today and you tell me a story?'

'I think we might,' answered the dragon. 'I was only thinking yesterday that I might tell you a giant story.'

'A giant!' echoed Susan. 'Have you seen giants?'

'Lots of 'em in my time,' answered the dragon, carelessly polishing his claws with a lump of seaweed, as he spoke. 'Cornwall was full of giants. I knew many of them. Used to give 'em rides on my back when they were children. My word, how they did pull my ears! I can feel it now.'

'Are you really going to tell me a story about a giant?'

'I could tell you dozens. There was Gog Magog, for instance, and there was Giant Bolster, who was twelve miles high and covered six miles in every step, and there was Blunderbore – I never cared much for him. But I think I won't tell you about a Cornish giant. There are lots of other stories. When you are older, be sure you go travelling, and when you are in foreign countries, ask people to tell you stories, then you will never be dull in the long winter evenings, for when the English stories run out, you will have all the other ones to tell.'

'Where did you hear this one?' asked Susan. 'In India? Or Honolulu? Or Timbuctoo?'

'Well, no. As a matter of fact, I have never been to those places,' said the dragon, blushing a little. He was, to tell the truth, rather a stay-at-home creature and had hardly ever been outside the British Isles. 'I heard this story, as far as I can remember, in Scotland.'

'People wear kilts in Scotland,' observed Sue, hoping she was telling the dragon something that he did not know.

'I wore one,' he answered calmly. 'There was a whole dragon clan living up in Scotland in those days. They taught me to dance reels. But it's the stories I remember most. Wonderful stories that went on and on for hours, and even days. We only used to interrupt them to eat a meal and perhaps get the stiffness out of our legs by dancing a few reels and strathspeys.'

'Is this story – the one you're going to tell me – a very long one?' asked Susan rather anxiously. 'I mean, will it go on for hours and hours, or – or even days and days, because, you know –'

'Don't be alarmed,' answered the dragon, kindly. 'It's one of the shorter ones. It's the tale of Molly Whuppie and how she got the better of a giant, which is a very difficult thing to do.

'Molly Whuppie was one of three sisters, the daughters of a poor couple, and they weren't the only children, either. There were several sons as well. As the children grew older, they ate more and more, and it cost so much to feed them and so much to clothe them, that the wretched mother and father just didn't know where the next penny was coming from. So at last they decided to take the three girls away to the forest and leave them there.

'"At least," said the father and mother to each other, "there may be enough food then for the rest of the children, whereas if we keep our three daughters, we may all of us die of hunger." '

'It was rather cruel of them, wasn't it?' said Susan, sorrowfully.

'Perhaps it was,' said the dragon, 'but they were so very, very poor, it seemed the only thing to do. And it all turned out for the best as you will see.

'The three girls wandered about in the dark forest for many hours after their parents had left them, and at last, seeing a house with lighted windows, they went up and knocked on the door. A great ugly old woman opened it.

'"Please, ma'am," said the eldest girl, dropping a curtsy as she'd been taught, "would you be kind enough to give us a bite of something to eat?"

'"Oh, no, my dears," she answered. "I couldn't do that. My husband is a giant. If he found you here, as like as not he'd eat you for his own supper."

'The girls began to cry, and the old woman thought to herself that it was a pity to turn them away, for her husband might be rather pleased to have three nice, tasty young girls for a meal, instead of the everlasting mutton and beef, so she changed her mind, and asked them in. When they had each eaten a bowl of bread and milk, she hid them in a cupboard. A little later, in came her husband.

" *Fee, fi, foh, fum!* " he bellowed,
" *I smell the blood of some earthly one.* "

'After supper, the giant's wife told her husband she had a surprise for him, whisked open the cupboard door, and showed him the three girls.

'"Aha!" cried the giant, and he and his wife laughed very heartily. "Put them to bed with our three dear small daughters, good wife, and in the morning – let me see – I'll give them each a penny and put them on their road to the nearest town." And then he whispered to his wife, and laughed in a most unpleasant way.

'Now the youngest of the three, Molly Whuppie, was a sharp-eared and sharp-witted girl. She heard most of what the giant and his wife had whispered to each other, in between their laughing, and she knew that in the night he meant to kill them, and have them served up for his breakfast. When they were all three in bed, with the giant's three ugly daughters, all of them packed like sardines into one great four-poster bed, the giant came in, and as he kissed each of his daughters good-night, he put round their necks chains of gold. Then he patted the heads of the three homeless girls, and round their necks he put three pieces of rope.'

'Why did he do that?' asked Susan.

'He wanted to be able to feel in the dark which was which,' answered the dragon, 'and his own daughters, though they were very young, were already about the same size as Molly and her sisters. He would know his own daughters, even in the dark, by their gold chains, you see. Molly Whuppie guessed this, for, as I said, she was a sharp-witted little thing. When the giant's daughters were asleep and snoring, she took off the gold chains and put them round the necks of herself and her sisters, and in exchange, she slipped the ropes round the necks of the giant's daughters. Sure enough, in the dead of night, the giant came creeping in. He felt round the necks of the girls, found the ropes, and dragged his three daughters out of bed and killed them, thinking they were Molly and her two sisters.

'"Aha!" laughed he. "There's my breakfast." And off he went, back to bed.

'Then Molly woke up her sisters.

'"Come," she said. "We must hurry away!" And all three of them crept out of the house and sped away as fast as they could. When daylight dawned, they found themselves on the outskirts of a town, and right in the centre of it stood the King's palace. In went Molly and her sisters, and straight up to the King himself.

'"It's a terrible thing," said she, "that you should allow such a wicked giant to live in your kingdom. Here's myself and my two sisters were almost eaten up by him for his breakfast."

'The poor King looked sadly at them.

'"Alas!" said he. "I know this giant only too well, but how can I get rid of him?"

'"First," said Molly Whuppie, "you must get rid of his

sword. And I will get it for you, if you will promise me a reward."

'"Indeed, I will," cried the King eagerly. "Your reward shall be that your eldest sister shall marry my eldest son."

'"Agreed!" says Molly Whuppie, and off she went, and this is how she won the giant's sword.

'She crept into the giant's house and hid under the bed. His great sword always hung at the head of his bed. Once he was asleep, she stole the sword, and carrying it as carefully as she could, she crept out of the room. But it was almost too big for her to carry, and she banged it against the floor. Up jumped the giant and off the two of them went – Molly just keeping ahead of the giant by reason of the quickness of her thin little legs. Soon she came to a very narrow bridge, called the Bridge of One Hair. Over it she ran, but the giant was too big to squeeze across it. He shook his fist at her, but she only laughed, and called out:

> *"Twice again, old Fi Foh Fee,*
> *I shall come to trouble ye."*

'Great was the rejoicing at the palace when the King received the giant's sword from Molly Whuppie. He kept his promise and married his eldest son to Molly's eldest sister.

'Next Molly made him promise that if she could get the giant's purse, which lay under his pillow, her second sister should be married to the King's second son.

'Off she went, and as before, she hid herself under the giant's bed, and once he was asleep and snoring like

twenty pigs, she reached up her hand, and felt for the
purse. There it was, round and hard, stuffed with stolen
guineas, no doubt. Molly soon had it out from under
the pillow, and off she ran. But this time she stumbled and
fell just as she got to the door, and the giant woke up and
was after her in a moment. Molly ran as fast as her legs
could carry her and the giant bounded behind her,
grunting and puffing like a hippopotamus. Soon she came
to the Bridge of One Hair, and she was over in a flash,
and there was the giant stuck on the far side, because he
was too big to squeeze across. Molly laughed merrily back
at his furious face and called out:

> " *Once again, old Fi Foh Fee,*
> *I shall come to trouble ye.*"

'Well, the King kept his promise and Molly's second
sister was married to the King's second son, and there was
great merrymaking at the palace.

'The King then said to Molly: "My dear, you're a
wonderful girl and there is nothing I should like better
than to see you married to my youngest son, but first
you must get the ring from off the giant's finger."

'This was a very difficult thing for Molly to do, but
she was not one to give up. Off she went, and once again
she hid beneath the giant's bed. After a while he came up
to bed, and was soon snoring and puffing like a crocodile
in a swamp. His hand slipped over the edge of the bed
and hung down beside Molly's head so that she could
see the thick gold ring on his finger. Slowly, very slowly,
she pushed and pulled at it, and little bit by little bit it
began to slip down the giant's finger. At last the ring

came off, but alas, the giant woke at the final tug and grabbed Molly's hand.

'"Ho! Ho!" he shouted. "I've caught you, Molly Whuppie. I've caught you!"

'He glared down at Molly Whuppie, over the edge of the bed.

'"Now," he muttered to himself. "What shall I do with you, eh, Miss Molly Whuppie? What shall I do with you?"

'Molly thought quickly and then she said:

'"If I were you, sir, this is what I'd do."

'"Oh?" says the giant. "Go on, Miss Molly Whuppie."

'"I'd put me into yon great leather bag that hangs over by the door, and I'd tie me up in it with a cat and dog and a needle and thread and a pair of scissors."

'"Well," said the giant. "What next?"

'"I'd go out into the woods, and cut the biggest stick I could see and come back and bang me with it," said Molly Whuppie.

'The giant thought this a huge joke.

'He slapped his thigh with a noise like a thunder clap, grabbed tight hold of Molly, and popped her into the leather bag, added a cat, a dog, a needle and thread, and a pair of scissors, and hooked the bag over a nail on the wall. Then he took his knife and went out to cut a big stick.

'As soon as he was gone, Molly called the giant's wife.

'"Oh, mistress giant," said Molly, sighing heavily. "Oh, if only you could see what I can see in here. Oh, my goodness, if *only* you could see it!"

'"What can you see?" demanded the giant's wife, full

of curiosity, thinking it might be something worth having.

'"Oh, my! Oh, my!" called Molly Whuppie. "It's wonderful the things you can see in here. You'd never believe."

'Of course the giant's wife was longing to see these wonderful things, so Molly cut a hole in the bag with the scissors, and got out. The giant's wife climbed in, and in a trice, Molly had sewn up the hole with the needle and thread. She had just finished when back came the giant, brandishing a huge stick. With a bellow of rage, he rushed up to the bag and began banging away at it with his stick. The giant's wife shrieked out that it was his own wife, not Molly Whuppie, in the bag, but the cat and dog made such a howling and screeching that the giant couldn't hear a word she said.

'Meanwhile, Molly slipped away and ran back to the King's palace. She handed over the giant's ring. The King kept his promise and everybody in the land was delighted when Molly Whuppie was married to the King's youngest son. As for the giant, now he had lost his sword, his purse and his ring, he had no more power left, and he never did another wicked deed. He just lived quietly in his house, and people gradually forgot all about him. But everybody remembered and loved brave Molly Whuppie, who had saved them and their children from the power of the cruel giant and his wicked wife.

'And that's all for today,' ended the dragon. 'I'm worn out – right out.' He eyed Sue hopefully. 'Almost faint, I am. I suppose – you haven't – got anything that – that would revive me?'

'A bun?' suggested Susan.

'Well, that would be a help,' said the dragon. 'Only if you happen to have one to spare, of course.'

'Silly old dragon! I've got a bun for you, and it's a sugar one today. Mummy gives me two now.'

She took the bun out of her pocket.

'Oh!' she cried, 'I've got a biscuit, too. I never ate it. I quite forgot.'

She was just about to bite into it when she saw the dragon's eyes looking sorrowfully at her biscuit, which was a digestive one.

'Would you like it as well?' she asked.

'Oh, I would,' said the dragon. 'I would indeed. After all, I have told you a good giant story.'

'Yes, you have,' agreed Susan. 'So please do have the biscuit as well. I ought to be getting back,' she added, thinking to herself that if it wasn't too near dinner time, her mother might give her another biscuit to make up for the one the dragon was eating.

'Is there a new dragon-charming song, or shall I use one of the old ones?'

'Let's have a new one,' suggested the dragon, in a crumby sort of voice, speaking through the digestive biscuit.

'Excuse me,' he added politely, and chewed and swallowed before he went on speaking. 'I'll send it to you, under your pillow.'

'How do you get them there?' asked Susan.

'Aha!' said the dragon. 'The same way Father Christmas puts things into your stocking, perhaps. Anyway, it's my secret.'

CHAPTER EIGHT

Under the Stars

UNFORTUNATELY, the next day started off very wet, and Susan could not go out at all in the morning. But it never rains all day in Cornwall. If it's wet in the morning, it will nearly always be fine in the afternoon or evening, and, sure enough, after lunch the rain stopped. There was still rather a lot of cloud in the sky, and Sue's mother did not think it a very good idea to go to the dragon's cave.

'Maybe he gets rheumatism in wet weather, and won't want to come out,' she suggested.

But Susan was determined to go.

She called the dragon out with a new dragon-charming song that she had found under her pillow:

> ' O where and O where is my dragon gone?
>   O where and O where is he?
> With his ears cut short and his tail cut long,
>   O dragon, come back to me!'

She soon saw his glowing, lamp-like eyes coming down the cave towards her.

'Not a very nice day,' he observed, looking up at the sky.

'No, it isn't,' agreed Susan, 'and Mummy's afraid you may have rheumatism.'

'Oh,' said the dragon. 'Well, as a matter of fact, I *have*.' Susan felt rather disappointed.

'Then I don't suppose you'll feel like going to that pool where Arthur found his sword?'

'I'd rather not, just today,' answered the dragon, working his left leg up and down very stiffly. 'Can you hear my joints creaking?'

Susan could. They sounded like squeaky car brakes.

'I don't fancy that I could fly with this stiff leg,' he went on, looking very long-suffering. 'But never mind. Looking forward to things is always the best part. If we'd gone to Dozmarie Pool today, then we shouldn't be able to look forward to going there tomorrow, should we?'

Susan didn't altogether agree with the dragon, but she could see that he really was rather rheumaticky and stiff.

'We *will* go tomorrow, won't we?' she begged. 'You see, we haven't got many more days here.'

'Haven't you?' The dragon looked rather gloomy. 'Dear, dear, I shall miss you.'

He sniffed, and then, wishing perhaps to change this painful subject, he said severely, pointing with his claw:

'You've a dirty mark on your face.'

'Have I?' Susan put her hand guiltily to her face and wiped at her cheek.

'It's on the other side,' said the dragon, watching her.

'Lower down. No. Now higher up. That's got it. Haven't you washed your face this morning?'

'Of course.'

'I thought I observed the same mark on your cheek yesterday.'

'It must have been a different one,' retorted Sue, 'because I know I washed. Last night and this morning.'

'Perhaps your mother didn't notice it. Maybe your mother is one of these lazy, courseying, couranting women, as they say in Cornwall.'

'Oh, she's not!' cried Sue. 'How can you say such things. You are horrid, dragon.'

'Come, come,' said the dragon. 'How do I know what your mother is like? I have never met her.'

'She's beautiful and quite, quite clean,' said Susan, indignantly.

'Good,' said the dragon. 'Don't take on so. Don't be offended.'

But Sue was cross with him. 'I don't think I'll stay with you this afternoon,' she said. 'Perhaps Mother would like me to go for a walk on the sand dunes with her.'

'Your mother wouldn't like that at all,' answered the dragon at once. 'Something tells me that she is very busy doing the family washing at this moment, which she couldn't do this morning because it was wet.'

Susan looked very surprised.

'As a matter of fact, she is. However did you know, dragon?'

'Oh, I just felt it in my bones,' he answered. 'Now, sit down and lend me your handkerchief and I'll wipe the dirt off your face.'

The dragon took Sue's handkerchief in his paw, licked a corner of it with his long, pink tongue, and rubbed Sue's cheek.

'There!' he said, handing back the handkerchief.

'Do you wash *your* face every morning?' asked Sue, gazing hard at the dragon.

'Always,' he answered. 'In the dew. *And* I have a bath most nights.'

'Where's your bathroom? In the cave?'

'No. I generally have my baths in a rock pool up there,' answered the dragon, pointing towards the rocks. 'Under the stars. I lie on my back and gaze up at them. It makes bathing a pleasure.'

'Oh!' cried Sue. 'I do wish Mother would let me do that. You are lucky, dragon. I've hardly ever seen the stars, but I expect I shall see them more when I grow up.'

'You won't,' retorted the dragon. 'You'll be too busy sleeping, like all humans. They sleep and sleep and sleep. I never knew such creatures. Almost as bad as cats. You never see anything worth seeing if you're always asleep.'

'But don't you ever want to sleep?' asked Susan.

'Oh, I snooze a bit during the day-time. I haven't much else to do. At night I go for walks along the beach and the cliffs. It's quiet and peaceful then. I'm not likely to meet anybody, and if I do, I just freeze and they think I'm a rock.'

'I wonder,' said Susan, 'if I could wake up and go out and look at the stars one night.'

'You could, if you wanted to badly enough.'

'I might be frightened. I wish you could be there, too, dragon.'

'I expect I could,' said the dragon, as if it were the

easiest thing in the world. 'Which is your cottage?'

Susan explained that it was the white one on the first corner up the lane from the beach.

'All right,' said the dragon, cheerfully, as though getting little girls out of bed to look at the stars was something he did quite often and was practised in.

'Tonight?' asked Susan.

'Why not?' answered the dragon. 'It's turned out fine. It's going to be a beautiful warm night.'

'But how shall I wake up?'

'I'll teach you a piece of magic. You must say it tonight before you go to sleep, and I can promise you you'll wake up and find me waiting for you just outside the window, so you needn't feel frightened.'

'Oh!' said Susan, rather breathlessly, feeling that she couldn't draw back. 'Suppose Mummy or Daddy wake up?'

'They won't,' said the dragon. 'I'll breathe a spell in at their window as I go by. Now listen. As you go back to your cottage, pick a blossom of an evening primrose – you know those tall, pale-yellow flowers up the lane? You do? Right. Pick just one blossom, and put it under your pillow. When your dear mother has tucked you up for the night, take it out and hold it in your hand, very gently, and say to it:

> *Evening flower, awake at night,*
> *Wake me too in the clear moonlight.*

Can you remember that?'

> '*Evening flower, awake at night,*
> *Wake me too in the clear moonlight,*'

repeated Sue.

'Now you'd better go home,' said the dragon. 'I'll be there, and in any case there's nothing to be frightened of at night. It's the best time of all when you get to know it. There's a full moon just now, and everything will be as clear as daylight, only far more beautiful. I'll be there to hold your hand. Perhaps we'll even see a shooting star. I often see them.'

Susan went home rather dazed. She saw the evening primroses, their buds still folded and rather withered looking. She picked one and took it home. She often picked wild flowers, so her mother didn't think anything of her taking it back with her. She put it carefully in a cup of water by her bedside, thinking it would like that better than being stifled too long under the pillow. Later on, when she undressed, she found to her great joy that it had opened out into a pale-yellow flower, and seemed to be waiting for her. Once her mother had left her tucked up, she reached out for it.

> *'Evening flower, awake at night,*
> *Wake me too in the clear moonlight,'*

she whispered, and put it under her pillow. She fell asleep very quickly.

When she awoke, a honey-coloured light seemed to fill the room. She could see her toys, her torch, her pile of clothes, quite clearly. She pulled back the curtain and looked out of the window. The moon, like a plate of gold, was hanging in the sky. A voice said softly:

'Susan!'

'Dragon!' called Sue. 'I'll be out in a minute. I'll bring my torch.'

'Be quick!' called the dragon, 'and don't fall over anything.'

Not bothering to put on a dressing-gown, or slippers, Sue switched on her torch and crept out of the room, and along the dark passage to the kitchen. The clock was ticking so loudly it seemed a wonder that anyone could sleep through it. She had a little trouble with the doors. They were difficult to manage with a torch in one hand, and made a fearful noise, it seemed to her. But no one woke up, and at last she was out of the back door, standing in the cool, dewy grass, holding one of the dragon's paws.

'I brought one of my seaweed blankets,' said the dragon. 'I didn't want you to catch cold. I think you'd better wrap it round you. And here's a rug to sit on.'

He spread it out on the grass.

'You are thoughtful,' said Susan.

'So is everyone,' said the dragon, 'only their heads aren't always full of the right thoughts. A pity, but there it is.'

Susan wasn't really listening to him. The whole sky was full of stars, some fiercely bright, and wavering up and down like small flames, others tiny pinpricks of light. There were clusters in strange and beautiful patterns, six or seven here, two or three there, and little patches of tiny ones like a sprinkling of dust on the blue velvet of the sky.

'Have they all got names?' she asked at last.

'Well, I suppose most of them have,' answered the dragon. 'But of course I don't know all of them. There are so many, we'd better just look at a few. Let's look at the one called the Dragon.'

'Of course,' said Susan, who knew that the dragon loved talking about dragons better than anything else.

'Well, first of all, we'll find a very bright star, one of the most beautiful in the sky. It's called Arcturus, and it's reddish gold in colour. Can you see it?'

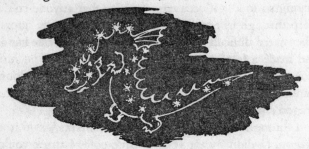

The dragon pointed with his paw, and Sue followed his direction. After gazing hard for a few moments, she could see one star brighter than the rest and deep golden.

'Now,' said the dragon, 'just above that (he waved his paw) are some stars shaped like a saucepan – got them? The Dragon is next door to it – three stars together and then a long, wavy tail.'

It was rather difficult to separate the Dragon from the other stars but at last Susan could make out its shape.

'Was it a nice Dragon?' she asked.

'Well, not very. In fact, it was rather a wicked creature.'

'Like you were once?'

'Worse – far worse. It ate people by the dozen. It lived in the sea, and used to pounce on to dry land and carry people off and eat them. In the end, the King of the country asked the gods how he could get rid of this terrible creature, and they said, only by giving up his own daughter, Andromeda. The King must tie her to a rock, and when the monster had eaten her, it would be satisfied (since she was a princess and tasted better than any ordinary person) and would go away and leave them in peace. The King was heart-broken, but he did as the gods commanded. He chained his daughter Andromeda to a rock, and sat alone in his palace, weeping, as he thought of her terrible fate.'

'I believe I know this story,' said Susan. 'A prince came and rescued her. Mummy told me.'

'Ah,' said the dragon. 'I'm glad you know *something*. Yes, a prince came and rescued her. His name was Perseus, and he was riding by through the air, on his winged horse, Pegasus. He spurred on his horse, and drew his sword, and rushed upon the sea monster, just as it was swimming through the waves towards Andromeda. After a terrible battle, he slew it. The sea was red with blood, and the creature had threshed about so much that it had raised a fearful storm and the waves were lashing round the poor girl as she lay on the rocks. But Perseus reached down and broke her chains, put her upon his winged horse and carried her back to her father's palace. Her father was so overjoyed, that he gave Andromeda to Perseus as his wife, as a reward for his brave deed. And then, later on, the gods put Perseus and Andromeda into the sky, and the winged horse, Pegasus, as well. They're over there,' said the dragon pointing, 'but you can't make them out very well. However, you *can* see the Dragon. He was put into the sky too.'

'I don't think he deserved to be,' said Susan, severely.

'No, he didn't really. But there he is.'

'What about the saucepan?' asked Sue. 'However did a saucepan get into the sky?'

'Well, it's not really a saucepan,' answered the dragon. 'It's rather a tiresome thing, because it's got so many names. Some people call it the Great Bear, and others call it Charles's Wain, but its real name is the Plough.'

'Tell me about it.'

'You won't remember if I tell you too many stories,' said the dragon.

'Well, *you* seem to remember them.'

'Ah, but I've known them for several hundred years, and in any case, I'm a – oh, there's a shooting star! Quick! Did you see it?'

'Oh, I saw it! I saw it!' cried Sue, jumping up from the seaweed rug in her excitement, and running over the dewy grass. 'It was beautiful – like a rocket. What happened to it?'

'I suppose it just went out,' answered the dragon. 'Like a candle – PUFF!'

He blew through his nose, and a little wreath of warm smoke rose in the still night air. He looked anxiously at Susan.

'Do come back on the rug,' he said. 'You *are* warm, aren't you? Just wearing that funny white nightie. I don't think you ought to stay out much longer.'

'All right, I won't. But it's so lovely out here. I never dreamt it would be so glorious,' said Susan.

'I knew you'd like it,' said the dragon. 'For a human child who was *not* brought up at the court of King Arthur, I must say you have most of the right ideas. Oh – KER-CHOO-OO!'

The dragon sneezed violently, shut his eyes tight and held out a paw in Sue's direction.

'Handkerchief! Handkerchief!' he snuffled.

'Oh, dear!' said Susan. 'I hope I've got one. Yes, here you are – ' and she pulled one out of her nightie pocket – 'Don't say *you're* catching cold. Perhaps I'd better go in now. It has been lovely. Oh! Oh! Another shooting star!'

A bright, reddish pinpoint of light slid across the sky, from one side to the other.

'Now I don't mind going in,' said Susan. She folded up the blanket and draped it over the dragon's back.

'Good night, dear dragon,' she said, and placed a kiss upon his cold, scaly cheek.

'Good night,' said the dragon. 'I've done many strange things in my time, but one thing I've never done before – shown the stars to a little girl in a white nightie.'

He stood and watched while Susan opened the back door and crept quietly in, and then he padded round the cottage and peered in at her window.

'All right?' he asked. 'Not cold?'

'Not now,' said Susan, pulling the bed-clothes round her.

'Good night, dragon, and thank you, *thank* you.'

'It's good morning now,' answered the dragon, and waved a paw through the window.

CHAPTER NINE

Childe Roland to the Dark Tower Came

Susan didn't see the dragon for two days, as it rained too hard to go to the beach, and when it did clear up, her mother and father took her off for picnics to other beaches. When at last she went down to the cave, and sang her dragon-charming song he did not appear. She knew he was there, as she could see a small spiral of smoke coming out from the cave, but when she called out: 'R. Dragon!' several times, and he still did not come, she knew he was cross, so she decided to play a game with herself till he felt more friendly. It had turned hot again, and the sand was warm to her bare feet. She picked up a long streamer of seaweed and ran along, floating it out behind her like a flag. She found herself running in a big circle, round and round a black, knobbly rock that stuck out of the sand, and as she ran, she waved the seaweed up and down. Perhaps it was the strong sun, perhaps it was running round and round in a circle, but suddenly she began to feel very odd. The rock in the middle of her circle looked horribly black. It had a high, pointed crown, rather like a witch's hat, and its lower jags and ledges were growing every minute more and more like the folds and pleats of a witch's skirt. She began to feel frightened. The rock looked almost as if it were moving.

'Dragon! R. Dragon!' called out Sue, breathlessly. 'Oh, I do wish you were here! Do come!'

A puff of green smoke appeared over the top of the rock and the dragon's head peered round it, his large fore-paws resting on what had looked so like the witch's shoulders.

'What's the matter?' asked the dragon.

'Oh, I'm so glad to see you, dragon,' cried Sue, running to him. 'That awful rock! It looked so – so horrid. Just like a witch.'

'You're a very silly little girl,' said the dragon, severely. 'I looked out of my cave, and there you were running round that rock *widdershins*. You must never do that.'

'Widdershins? Whatever is that?' asked Susan.

'The wrong way,' said the dragon.

'But what is the wrong way round? I don't see how there can be a right and wrong way round an old rock.'

'Indeed?' said the dragon. 'There is a right and a wrong way round anything.'

'Oh,' said Susan, doubtfully. 'Well, anyway, dragon, you might tell me what that queer word means.'

'Widdershins?'

'Yes, widdershins. What is it?'

'It means going from the right to the left, the *wrong* way, the opposite way to the sun. You watch the sun and you'll see it goes through the sky from left to right. Look, it rises, doesn't it, roughly over Trevose Head?'

'Yes,' said Sue, looking towards the lighthouse.

'And it sets there, over the sea. Well?'

'Well, what's wrong about widdershins, anyway?' asked Susan.

'It's the way the witches go round,' said the dragon. 'Witches and all bad creatures.'

'Have you ever run in a circle that way?'

'I?' asked the dragon, huffily. 'Certainly not. At least,' he added, blushing, 'not since the days I was bad and ate maidens in distress.'

'Is that why the rock looked so like a witch? When I was running round it widdershins?'

'That's why. Now we'll sit on this silly old witch, and I'll tell you a story about a girl who ran widdershins, and you'll see what happened to her, and then perhaps you'll be more careful in future. Though you don't deserve a story,' added the dragon, frowning, 'because you haven't been to see me for three days.'

'Two days and a half,' corrected Susan. 'I saw you last in the middle of Tuesday night.'

'Ah,' said the dragon. 'That was exciting. I enjoyed that. Did you wake up very late in the morning?'

'Yes,' answered Susan, 'and Mummy and Daddy were terribly surprised when I told them about the stars. They thought I had got it all from school, but of course they don't teach you things as exciting as stars at school.'

'I can't think what they do teach,' remarked the dragon, sorrowfully. 'Nothing that is worth knowing, as far as I can make out.'

Susan did not altogether agree with him, but she didn't say anything because the dragon didn't like being disagreed with. They sat down on a comfortable ledge of the rock, and the dragon curled his tail round a knob, so that it looked like a long green piece of seaweed.

'There was once a handsome young man called Childe Roland,' he began, 'who lived with his two brothers and his sister, whose name was Burd Helen.'

'Bird?' said Susan. 'What a funny name.'

'Spelt a different way, – BURD,' explained the dragon, kindly. 'It means fair, beautiful. Really, you modern children know nothing. Their father was dead, and their mother brought them up as best as she could in a small cottage. One day, Roland and his brothers were playing football and Roland, who was very strong, kicked the football so hard that it flew over the church tower. His sister, Helen, cried: "I'll run and get it!" and off she went, running round the church, *widdershins* – the wrong way of the sun, so that her shadow fell behind her. She never came back. A day passed. A week passed. The brothers searched and searched for her, but they never found her. A month went by and a year, and the eldest brother, whose name I don't know –'

'Let's call him Jeremy,' suggested Susan, who had a friend of this name.

'All right – Jeremy went to Merlin, the great magician.

'"Merlin!" he cried, bowing very low. "I have come to ask you if you will help me find my dear sister Burd Helen, who has been missing from home for a year and a day, and the hearts of my poor widowed mother and of myself and my two brothers are breaking, for we loved her very dearly."

'Then he told Merlin the story of the football going over the church.

'"It is plain to me," said Merlin slowly, "that she must have run round the church widdershins, so that her shadow fell behind her, and the King of Elfland caught her by her shadow, and has stolen her away. If you want to find her, you must go to Elfland."

'And then Merlin explained how he was to find the way.

'"You must go by this road and that road, and over this hill and that hill, and through this valley and that valley. Take your sword, and cut off the head of any creature that speaks to you. If you want to get home safely, eat nothing and drink nothing. Remember my words."

'Away went Jeremy. But he never came back. A week passed. A month passed. A year. But he did not return, so the next brother went off to seek Merlin.'

'What was his name?' asked Susan.

'I really don't remember,' said the dragon. 'But names are important, so you choose one.'

'Stephen,' said Sue.

'All right, Stephen,' said the dragon. 'Away went Stephen to visit Merlin, the great magician.

'"Merlin!" he cried, bowing very low. "I have come to ask you if you will help me to find my dear sister Helen, and my brother Jeremy, who have been from home for many months, and the hearts of my poor widowed mother and of myself and of my brother Roland are breaking, for we loved them very dearly."

'"Your brother is gone to Elfland to seek your sister Helen," answered Merlin, "and it is plain to me that he

has not remembered my words. If you want to find them,
you also must go to Elfland, and I will explain to you
how to find the way. You must go by this road and by
that road, and over this hill and that hill, and through
this valley and that valley. Take your sword and cut off
the head of any creature that speaks to you. If you want to
get home safely, eat nothing and drink nothing. Remember my words."

'Stephen thanked Merlin and went away. But he never
came back. A week passed. A month. A year. But he did
not return. Then Childe Roland buckled on his father's
sword and set out to visit Merlin. And before he could
greet him, Merlin cried:

'"You are Childe Roland, come to seek your sister
Burd Helen, and your brothers Jeremy and Stephen."

'"I am," answered Roland, bowing low.

'"They are in Elfland," said Merlin, "but I need not
tell you the way, for you are wearing your father's sword,
and that gives you knowledge of the fairy places. I will
only give you one piece of advice: cut off the head of any
creature that speaks to you, and eat nothing and drink
nothing. Remember my words."

'"I will remember them," answered Roland, and set
off. He travelled far and wide, seeking Elfland. At last he
came to it, and he knew it at once, because the grass was
greener than anywhere else, and the air tasted quite
different.'

'How did it taste?' interrupted Susan.

'A taste that is a mixture of sweet and bitter,' answered
the dragon. 'You cannot describe it, but you would know
it at once if you breathed it. Roland saw a herd of small,
shaggy ponies, with fiery eyes, that glowed like lamps in

their heads, and they were guarded by a small, wizened old man, whose eyes shone yellow like a cat's.

'"You must be the King of Elfland's horse-herd," cried Roland. "Tell me, where is the Dark Tower of the Elf King?"

'The horse-herd looked at Roland up and down with his cat's eyes, and answered: "Go on till you come to the King of Elfland's cow-herd. He will know."

'Roland turned away to go, when he remembered Merlin's words. He whipped out his sword and with one stroke cut off the horse-herd's head. And the horse-herd picked it up, with its yellow cat's eyes still gleaming, tucked it under one arm, and went on with his work.

'Roland travelled further till he came to a herd of small, shaggy cattle. They were guarded by a man dressed all in green, with a hard, stern face as bleak as a winter's day.

'"You must be the King of Elfland's cow-herd," said Roland. "Tell me, where is the Dark Tower of the Elf King?"

'The cow-herd looked Roland up and down with his hard little eyes, and answered: "Go on till you come to the King of Elfland's henwife. She will know."

'And Roland drew his sword, and cut off the cow-herd's head, and the cow-herd picked it up, tucked it under his arm and melted away like November mist.

'Roland travelled on, till he came to a brood of chickens, guarded by a little old woman, and her eyes were like pale, rain-washed pebbles.

'"You must be the King of Elfland's hen-wife," cried Roland. "Tell me, where is the Dark Tower of the Elf King?"

'And the henwife looked him up and down with her

pebble eyes, and she pointed with her skinny finger and answered: "There!"

'Roland was so overjoyed that he forgot to cut off her head, and turned away, when he heard behind him a tiny, thin, cackle of laughter. At once he whipped round, drew out his sword, and cut off her head.

'Before him he saw the Dark Tower of the Elf King, and he ran swiftly round it three times, widdershins, holding his bright sword in his hand. Then he cried loudly: "Open door!"

'A door in the gloomy tower swung open. Inside, all was as light as day, and there stood his sister, Burd Helen, crying: "Welcome, brother!"

'With one stroke of his sword, Roland swept off her head. The tower shook, all went black for a moment, and there was a terrible roll of thunder. Roland stood still, full of fear. But the next moment, the darkness cleared away, and there stood the real Burd Helen, alive and well, before him, and he caught her in his arms.

'When they had greeted each other, Childe Roland said: "I am weary. Dear Sister, fetch me food and drink, for I can do nothing more till I have eaten."

'Burd Helen did not speak, but she looked at her brother sorrowfully, as she fetched him a goblet of wine. He took it from her trembling hand, but as he raised it to his lips, he remembered the words of Merlin and flung the goblet to the ground.

'There was a sound of heavy footsteps, echoing through the halls of the Dark Tower, and the voice of the Elf King came to the ears of Childe Roland, as he stood by his sister.

> *"Fee, fi, foh, fum,*
> *I smell the blood of a Christian man.*
> *Be he alive or be he dead,*
> *I'll grind his bones to make my bread."*

'Roland cried: "Out, sword, out! Strike now or never again!"

'He rushed at the terrible Elf King, and for an hour and seven minutes they fought up and down the hall, their swords clashing and striking sparks off each other.

'At last the Elf King slipped on the wet flagstones, where the goblet of wine had been spilt, and as he lay on the ground, Childe Roland set his foot upon his throat and his sword point at his heart, and said:

'"King of Elfland, you shall go free only if you bring my brothers back to life and set my sister Helen free."

'And the King of Elfland groaned and said: "I will."

'He rose to his feet and brought out of a tall cupboard a crystal jar of clear red oil, and with this he anointed the hands and nostrils of Jeremy and Stephen, who were lying dead in a dark corner of the great hall. At once they rose and stretched their limbs and greeted their brother with joy.

'Still carrying the sword in his hand, Roland led the way from the Dark Tower, back through the green grass and the bittersweet air of Elfland, till they came to their own country at last, and to their widowed mother, who stood weeping at her gate, for she had thought that she would never see her sons and her daughter again.'

There was a long silence.

'Didn't you like the story?' asked the dragon. His voice sounded quite anxious.

'I loved it so much,' said Susan, 'I can't bear to remember it. Tell it to me all over again.'

'It's rather long,' said the dragon. 'Another day, perhaps.'

'That's the trouble,' sighed Susan. 'There aren't any more days, hardly. We go home the day after tomorrow.'

'Oh, dear,' said the dragon. 'Oh, dear, oh, dear. That's sad news.' He gave an unmistakable sniff.

'Are you going to miss me, dragon?' asked Susan.

'Perhaps I am,' he answered.

'So am I going to miss you,' said Susan. 'Terribly.'

'Never mind,' said the dragon, giving another sniff. 'There's next year to look forward to. You'll come and visit me then, won't you?'

'Oh, of course, I will!'

'Then, don't let's be dismal,' said the dragon. 'I'll be thinking up some new stories to tell you next year.'

'And I'll be thinking up some to tell you,' said Susan, adding, 'only nothing I could think of would be so exciting and glorious as the story of Childe Roland.'

She felt in her pocket and produced a bun.

'It's got sugar on it,' she said, and held it out to the

dragon. 'Tomorrow I'm going to bring you *two*, because it's the last day.'

She watched the dragon eating his bun, and then said good-bye to him and ran back over the rocks to Constantine Bay.

CHAPTER TEN

The Pool of Excalibur

The next morning, Susan thought she would try to make up a dragon-charming song of her own, as a surprise for the dragon, on this last day, so all through breakfast she muttered to herself, and the bacon grew cold, and her mother quite cross.

Her first two lines were:

> *'Puff, puff, dragon,*
> *Have you any smoke?'*

But she couldn't find a rhyme for the word 'smoke'. She could only think of 'coke', and 'broke', and 'woke', and none of them seemed to fit in. So she gave up that beginning and tried something else:

> *'Sing a song of dragons,*
> *A pocketful of buns.*

'What rhymes with buns?' she asked, despairingly.

'Tons,' said her father.

'Try ones,' said her mother. 'You know – different

kinds. What about "gingerbread and almond and chocolate ones"?'

'Lovely,' said Susan. 'How shall we go on? Like this?

> '*When the buns were eaten,*
> *The dragon gave a roar —*'

Susan's mother stopped eating her bread and marmalade and went on:

> '*So Susan's mother baked a batch,*
> *And then they had some more.*'

'Oh, I'm sure that will charm the dragon beautifully!' cried Susan. 'I'll go down directly after dinner, and sing it. D'you think I could take him a picnic, as it's the last day? He does so love picnics.'

'So do you,' said her mother. 'All right. I'll pack up one.'

So Susan practised her song nearly all the morning, while she was bathing and playing on the sand, till all the crabs in Constantine Bay knew it by heart too, and sang it to their crab children that night when they were rocking them to sleep in the pools.

After lunch, Susan ran down to Constantine Bay and as quickly as she could over the rocks to the dragon's cave. She stood outside and sang:

> '*Sing a song of dragons,*
> *A pocket full of buns,*
> *Gingerbread and almond*
> *And chocolate ones.*
> *When the buns were eaten*

The dragon gave a roar,
So Susan's mother baked a batch
And then they had some more.'

Out from the cave came floating a perfect green ring of smoke, quickly followed by the dragon himself.

'That was a very nice charming song,' he said. 'I believe you made it up. I don't seem to have heard it before.'

'I did make it up,' answered Susan, proudly. 'Mummy and Daddy helped me a bit, though.'

'Ah,' said the dragon, approvingly. 'I'm glad to learn that people can still make up poetry. It's a useful art. Now, what are we going to do today?'

'*You* know,' said Susan. 'We're going to the pool where Arthur found Excalibur. You promised as a good-bye present.'

'To Dozmarie Pool? Well, yes, so I did promise. Now Dozmarie Pool is a wild place. The Demon Tregeagle lived there in the old days. Indeed, I've heard it said that he's there still. I think I must put my teeth in.'

'Your teeth?'

'Yes. You may have noticed,' said the dragon, shyly, 'that I have no teeth.'

'It's one of the things I liked most about you,' said Susan, with enthusiasm.

'I don't need teeth now that I don't eat maidens tied to rocks and such-like things. Except for an occasional turkey – or two turkeys – at Christmas time, and a goose – or geese – at Whitsun, and chickens on my birthday, I eat mostly berries now, and bananas and bread and cheese and buns –'

'I've got some for today,' said Susan hastily, and the dragon heaved a sigh of relief and went on:

'I don't often need my teeth now, so I keep them in a box.'

'Are they false teeth?' asked Susan.

'Of course not,' retorted the dragon, indignantly. 'They're MY teeth. They live in here.'

He showed her a very long box, like a giant pencil box.

'Oh, do let me see you put them in!' cried Susan.

'No,' answered the dragon firmly. 'I do that in private.'

He retired behind a rock, and Sue could hear a loud, clicking noise, like a giant's wife knitting socks very rapidly on two pairs of needles. Then the dragon reappeared, looking rather fierce, with two rows of enormous teeth in his mouth.

'You wouldn't forget, would you, that you don't eat maidens any more?' asked Sue, anxiously.

'Oh, dear, no,' answered the dragon, smiling and revealing even more teeth. 'Oh, dear me, no. They wouldn't agree with me. They'd give me dreadful indigestion. Shall we go now?'

'Let's,' said Sue.

'All right, then,' said the dragon. 'Climb on my back, and hold on tight. NOW – I'm for Dozmarie Pool!'

'I'm for Dozmarie Pool!' shrieked Sue. There was a

whirring of wings and a rush of air. She looked down and
saw the beach vanishing away behind them. Soon they
were over the river at Padstowe. It wound through the
green countryside like a snake.

'There is Bodmin Moor,' shouted the dragon, pointing
an outstretched claw towards purple hills.

They were flying very fast, and the wind rushed past
Susan's ears and made it difficult to hear.

'What did you say?' she called.

'Bodmin Moor!' bellowed the dragon. 'Down below
us now.'

It seemed only a few minutes before he was slowing
down, and they came gently to the ground, on the
heather.

'Here we are,' said the dragon. 'Sometimes, I feel I
should like to come and live here. This is just my sort of
country. Heather and rocks, and very few people, and
lovely brown streams to drink out of.'

'Why don't you?' asked Susan. 'I'd love to come and
stay with you here.'

'Well,' answered the dragon, slowly, 'I do like the
sea. I'd miss the sea badly.'

'You could always go to the sea when you wanted
to.'

'I don't like visiting places. I like to live in them. In
the old days this was a favourite place for dragons. Many
of them my friends and relations.'

The dragon stopped speaking and two fat tears rolled
down his cheeks.

'All gone,' he said, sadly.

'Poor dragon,' said Sue, who was a very sympathetic
child. 'Poor dragon. Shall I lend you a handkerchief?'

'Only if it's a big one,' said the dragon.

'It isn't a big one,' said Susan, 'but I happen to have two. I've still got yesterday's with the lollipop in it that I didn't finish. One will do for each eye.'

The dragon applied the handkerchiefs, sniffing loudly, like the noise of a train going through a tunnel.

'Thank you,' he said. 'I feel better. I might feel better still if I ate the remains of the lollipop.'

'Do,' said Susan, politely, though she was longing to eat it herself.

The dragon put it in the corner of his mouth, and there was silence for a few minutes.

'All gone,' he said, with satisfaction. 'Now we'll find the pool. It's just over here.' And he set off down a narrow path through the heather.

After a few minutes they came to a hollow and below them lay the pool – a dark, still sheet of water, surrounded by the brown and purple hills. There was no one in sight, and not a ripple on the surface of the water.

'I think it's beautiful,' said Susan, 'but rather frightening.'

'Not with me here it isn't,' said the dragon, comfortingly. 'Sit on my back, and you'll feel safer. You'll see it better, too.'

Sue scrambled up on to the dragon's back and looked down into the still depths of the lake.

'It does look deep,' she said at last.

'People say it has no bottom,' said the dragon. 'Once, a thorn bush was thrown into it. It disappeared and months later it came up in Falmouth harbour, miles and miles away. It had gone by underground streams right across Cornwall.'

'Did King Arthur meet the Lady of the Lake again?' asked Sue. 'Here, at Dozmarie Pool?'

'I expect those books of yours tell you it wasn't here at all,' said the dragon, rather crossly. 'There are so many pools in England, and, of course, everyone wants his own favourite little pool to be the place, but I say it *was* here in Cornwall, and the answer is: yes, Arthur did meet the Lady of the Lake again, and not only her but her sisters. But it's a sad story. Do you mind sad stories?'

'I like them,' answered Sue. 'Even if they make me cry, I still like them.'

'Very right and proper,' said the dragon. 'Had I ever had a dragon daughter,' he went on, looking fondly at Susan, 'I should have wished her to be like you.'

Susan was very touched by this.

'Oh, Dragon –' she began.

'R. Dragon,' he corrected, stiffly.

'Will you ever tell me what R. stands for?' asked Susan.

'I believe I might,' said the dragon, unexpectedly. 'But first I'll tell you the story. When Arthur grew old, his own nephew, Mordred, whom he loved dearly, rose up against him, and slew many of his knights in battle. And at last their armies met at a place called Barham Down and there they fought till it was near night and a hundred thousand men lay dead upon the down. And Arthur, seeing Mordred leaning upon his sword to rest himself, took a spear and ran at his wicked nephew and drove his spear through his heart. But Mordred, before he fell, lifted up his sword, and smote Arthur's head and wounded him sorely. Of all Arthur's knights, only two were left, Sir Lucan and his brother, Sir Bedivere, and they were wounded almost to death. They carried the king away from the battlefield to the edge of this lake, and laid him down in the heather, and there Sir Lucan died. Then Arthur called to him the other knight, Sir Bedivere, and said:

'"My faithful Bedivere, take Excalibur, my good sword, and go with it to the waterside and throw my sword into that water and come again and tell me what you see."

'Now Bedivere looked at the sword, as he carried it to the edge of the lake, and he said to himself: "Surely it is shameful to cast away such a rich sword as this. The blade is as bright and keen as ever. I will not fling it away."

'So he hid it under a tree and went back to the king, and told him that he had thrown it into the water.

'"And what did you see?" asked King Arthur.

'"Sir," answered the knight, "I saw nothing but the waves and winds."

'"You are not speaking the truth," said Arthur, sinking back upon his couch of heather. "Take the sword and go again to the lake, and do as I bid you. Throw it in."

'So Sir Bedivere returned and took the sword Excalibur from its hiding-place, but again he could not bear to cast it away. So he hid it, even more carefully, and went back to the king.

'"Did you cast it into the lake?" asked Arthur.

'"Ay, my lord," answered Bedivere.

'"And what did you see?" asked the dying king.

'"Sir," answered the knight, "I saw nothing but the waves moving."

'"Alas," said the king. "I thought you were my faithful knight, but you are lying to me. Go back and do as I have commanded you, or I will slay you with my own hands."

'So a third time Sir Bedivere went back to the water's edge, and this time he threw the sword as far as he could into the middle of the pool, and as he watched in the twilight, a white hand and arm rose up above the water and caught the sword. Three times it waved Excalibur above the lake, and then it disappeared beneath the ripples with the sword, and the pool grew still and black.

'He returned and told the king what he had seen and Arthur cried: "That is well. Now carry me to the lake side."

'So Sir Bedivere took the king upon his back, and went with him to the waterside. And when they were there, there came in sight a little barge, with many fair ladies in it, and they wept when they saw King Arthur.

'"Now put me in the barge," said the king. So he did so, and the ladies, who were the ladies of the lake, took him into their care, and slowly the barge moved away from the waterside. And as Sir Bedivere watched in the growing darkness, it seemed to him that far away, like clouds, appeared a host of islands, and these were the islands of the blest, the fairest of which is called the Isle of Avalon. And there lives Arthur to this day, together with Merlin and all his knights who served him faithfully and died bravely in battle.'

'Is that the end of the story,' said Susan, after a pause.

'Yes,' said the dragon. 'And now, don't let's feel sad any more. Let's have our picnic.'

So they sat down beside the lake on a comfortable patch of heather and Susan undid the picnic basket. There were jam sandwiches, and two Swiss buns, a banana and a bottle of lemonade.

'Oh, dear, I do wonder how you will get on without

me,' sighed Susan, looking anxiously at the dragon as he nibbled his half banana.

'Don't worry,' he replied, cheerfully. 'I managed quite well for several hundred years. That's not to say I shan't miss you,' he added hastily, 'but you mustn't worry about me. Besides, we are going to meet again.'

'Yes, but next year you mightn't recognize me,' said Susan. 'I shall be ever so much bigger, I expect.'

'You just sing me that dragon-charming song you made up, the one you sang this morning. Then I shall know it's you.'

'And will you give my love to the mermaid next time you see her?'

'Of course.'

'Dragon?'

'Yes?'

'There's one thing more.'

'What is it?'

'What does R. stand for?'

'Well,' began the dragon, and stopped.

'Oh, why won't you tell me?'

'Names are so powerful,' said the dragon. 'There's no knowing what would happen if I told you.'

'You know *mine*,' objected Susan.

'Yes, but you're not a magical creature like I am. You see, if you tell a human your name, they have power over you. If you called out my real name, I'd have to come to you, no matter where you were. It might not be convenient. Suppose you were in the middle of an arithmetic lesson, and couldn't make the sum come right, you might be tempted to call out – well, to call out my name, and then I'd have to come. That's what human creatures do. They want the magic used for such silly things.'

'I'm not silly,' said Susan, crossly. 'I'd never call you just to do a stupid old sum. Besides, I could do it myself, I expect.'

'Well, yes, I dare say you could,' said the dragon. 'I will say you don't seem a stupid child.'

'If I promise never to call you by your name unless I *really* want you,' said Sue. 'Only if I were being chased by a bull, or falling off a roof or something?'

'What awful things you think of,' said the dragon, shuddering.

'Well, there you are,' said Susan, pleased to see that she was having some effect upon the dragon at last. 'You wouldn't like me to fall off a roof, would you? Or be chased by a bull?'

'I shouldn't like it at all,' said the dragon. 'Perhaps I *had* better tell you my name, if that's the sort of little girl you are, always climbing about on roofs, or running up against mad bulls.'

'There!' said Susan, triumphantly, 'and I *will* promise only to use it then. Or,' she added, as an afterthought, 'if a wolf tried to eat me.'

'I thought there weren't wolves in England any more,' said the dragon, rather uncertainly.

'Well, I haven't exactly seen any, but I expect there are some,' said Susan, boldly. 'And I might meet one.'

'All right, perhaps – I'm not making any promises, mind you, – *perhaps* I'll tell you,' said the dragon.

'Now?'

'No, not now. It might *just* be worth your while looking under your pillow tonight.'

'Where I used to find the dragon-charming songs?'

'Yes, but you mustn't be disappointed if there's nothing there. And now it's time we were getting back. Come on, climb up! Have you buried the bits of paper?'

For the last time, Susan climbed up on to the dragon's scaly back, and they said good-bye to Dozmarie Pool and Bodmin Moor, and started for home.

'Good-bye! Good-bye!' said Susan, softly, to herself, as they passed over the river at Padstowe, and then over the lighthouse at Trevose Head.

They landed in front of the dragon's cave, and Susan slipped off his back. She put her arms round as much of his neck as she could and kissed him.

'Good-bye, dragon,' she said, sadly. 'And thank you for all the stories, and for everything else, and specially for today.'

'Good-bye, Susan,' said the dragon. 'Wait a moment. I've got something for you.'

He disappeared into the cave for a moment, and then came out carrying a green handkerchief, the one with R.D. embroidered in the corner, in cowrie shells.

'For you to keep,' he said, handing it to Sue.

'Oh, thank you,' she said. 'Thank you, dear dragon. Will you keep mine, too?'

She pulled out her two handkerchiefs and selected the cleanest one. 'That one isn't sticky,' she said.

The dragon folded it carefully and held it in one paw. 'Now off you go,' he said briskly.

As Susan ran away across the sands, she looked back, and the dragon waved and blew her a green kiss which floated like a breath of smoke over the sands.

When she went to bed that night, she could hardly bear to look under her pillow. Suppose there was nothing there? Somehow Susan didn't believe that the dragon would disappoint her, so she took a deep breath and lifted the pillow. There lay a very small piece of yellowish paper and on it was written – one word. I can't tell you what the word was, for if I did, you would know the dragon's name, and you might try to call him to you and you will remember that that is exactly what he did not want to happen. But Sue read the word several times over, and went to sleep murmuring it to herself. When she looked for the piece of paper the next morning, while her father and mother were packing up the car to go home, it had vanished. But that didn't matter for she knew she would never forget the dragon's name.